I0817970

DON'T LOOK

(A Taylor Sage FBI Suspense Thriller —Book 1)

Molly Black

Molly Black

Debut author Molly Black is author of the MAYA GRAY FBI suspense thriller series, comprising six books (and counting); the RYLIE WOLF FBI suspense thriller series, comprising three books (and counting); and of the TAYLOR SAGE FBI suspense thriller series, comprising three books (and counting).

An avid reader and lifelong fan of the mystery and thriller genres, Molly loves to hear from you, so please feel free to visit www.mollyblackauthor.com to learn more and stay in touch.

ISBN: 978-1-0943-9392-6

BOOKS BY MOLLY BLACK

MAYA GRAY MYSTERY SERIES
GIRL ONE: MURDER (Book #1)
GIRL TWO: TAKEN (Book #2)
GIRL THREE: TRAPPED (Book #3)
GIRL FOUR: LURED (Book #4)
GIRL FIVE: BOUND (Book #5)
GIRL SIX: FORSAKEN (Book #6)

RYLIE WOLF FBI SUSPENSE THRILLER
FOUND YOU (Book #1)
CAUGHT YOU (Book #2)
SEE YOU (Book #3)

TAYLOR SAGE FBI SUSPENSE THRILLER
DON'T LOOK (Book #1)
DON'T BREATHE (Book #2)
DON'T RUN (Book #3)

PROLOGUE

Not a soul in sight. Perfect.

Chris's feet pounded the pavement, the early morning air prickly and cool in his lungs. A snake-like path wound through Ames Park—it was still dark enough for fog to obscure the playground's silhouette, but light enough for the rising sun's hues to work their way through the trees. Chris always liked watching the sky transform from denim blue to a wash of orange.

Crickets trilled from the grassy fields, and the sound of the lake trickled through the air. Ames Park was nestled between the lake and the town, divided by trees to create the illusion of running with nature. It worked—Chris felt one with the planet out here, rather than in the middle of a Northern Virginia town filled with six thousand busybodies.

When he'd moved to Lake Vernon from New York City, he'd hoped for the quiet serenity of an American small town. He wasn't warned about the nosy neighbors and people with too much time on their hands. He sighed as he ran, remembering a particularly unfortunate encounter with a customer at the hardware shop yesterday. In a couple hours, he'd have to do it all again: smile and nod, because the customer is always right.

Bullshit.

Chris continued up the path and tried to rinse the negativity away.

As he ran, a red figure appeared through the haze.

That's weird; no one's ever out here so early. He squinted as it became clearer.

A woman sat upright on a bench, posture rigid, back perfectly straight. She wore a bright red dress that stood out against the muted tones of the park. A straw hat rested on top of her head, tilted down to conceal her face with the brim. She looked like she'd fallen out of a high school prom set in a barnyard, but it wasn't anywhere near the end of the schoolyear; the town's teenagers should have all been safely asleep by then. Besides, this woman didn't look drunk or passed out—she resembled more of a monk meditating, if it weren't for her strange attire.

Chris jogged past. Not his business.

He had to hand it to the town's planners: this was a great park. As the sun peeked over the trees, its reflection rippled off the lake like a watercolor painting. It was smart to build a path right along the water, so the town's citizens—or at least, one of them—could appreciate it each day.

It took another half an hour to reach the end of the path, and Chris began to double back. Dawn had fully elapsed. He wished it would have lasted forever, that he didn't have to return to his mundane life. But it kept food on the table. That was all that mattered—keeping him and his girls healthy.

On his way back up the path, Chris approached the bench again. Even from afar, he could see the woman in the red dress was still there. He drew closer, until they were right next to each other.

It had been at least an hour since he'd first passed.

She hadn't moved an inch.

A bad feeling churned inside him. Chris had two daughters; he'd never been one to leave vulnerable young women where they could get hurt. Alone out here all night, she was lucky she hadn't been snatched up by some suburban predator.

Warily, he took a closer look. She was so still, stiller than the undisturbed lake behind him.

Is this even a person? Or is it a mannequin? Is this some sort of teenage prank?

Chris's palms grew sweaty. He needed to make a decision.

I'll just ask if she's fine. Be a good Samaritan.

"Excuse me, miss?" he asked delicately, like talking to a skittish animal. The last thing he wanted to do was make her think *he* was the danger.

No movement, no words. A crow squawked as it flew overhead.

"Hey, you should really wake up," he said, taking another step closer.

The woman's rather large feet were stuffed into black high heels, and her skin was chalky-pale. Thick, dark hair covered her thin legs, more leg hair than he'd ever seen on a woman. Her knees appeared chalky and dry, like they'd flake right off if he touched them.

And are those bruises?

"Hello?" Chris tried again. "Are you okay? Do you need me to call someone?"

His hand instinctively went for his phone as though it were a gun, tucked safely in the pocket of his running shorts. No response. Chris checked over his shoulder—they were still alone. Part of him wanted to bolt out of there, get some external help, but he quickly realized he was being ridiculous. She was just a woman, and she was in rough shape, so he had to help now.

"Miss, it isn't safe for girls to be out here all alone," Chris said. "If you need a ride home, I can help. I'm a friend. I have two girls myself."

Hesitantly, Chris touched her shoulder—but he was met with a stiff, ice-cold body. He accidentally shifted her, causing her head to fall limply to the side and the straw hat to tumble off.

Chris's blood went cold.

This was no woman at all.

A dead man with barely a hint of facial hair stared back at him, eyes open and devoid of life. Red lipstick was smeared across his face, and his mouth was taped back in a wide, sinister smile.

Chris screamed and jumped back. His phone fell and cracked against the concrete. As he fumbled to find it, he couldn't take his eyes off the dead man.

And he knew no amount of running would ever make him unsee this.

CHAPTER ONE

Just smile, no matter how much you want to run. Special Agent Taylor Sage put on her brave face as her husband closed the door to their new home.

"Well, honey, this is it," Ben let out a satisfied sigh.

Before meeting Ben, Taylor hadn't pictured herself 'settling down' in years. Not since she was a naïve junior agent fresh out of the FBI academy in Oregon. Sometimes, their peaceful life—their *happiness*—felt foreign to her, and the urge to run appeared again, beckoned her to disappear into the night. But she couldn't do that to Ben. Not again.

"Movers won't be here till tomorrow." He wrapped his arm around her shoulders, encasing her in warmth. Ben was easily the most handsome, endearing man she'd ever known—with his short brown hair and chocolate eyes, he never failed to make her heart melt. "What do you say we take a proper tour of our new home before it's filled with all our junk?"

"*Our* junk?" Taylor lifted a brow, and Ben laughed.

"Yes, Taylor. When you agreed to marry me, my junk became yours too." He winked as he slipped his hand into hers, dragging her into their open concept living room.

"Touché," Taylor mumbled.

Their last house in Portland had been Ben's first, and Taylor had moved in after their wedding. It had been a bit hard to separate what was his from hers; she'd never been one to carry much with her, but her husband was a borderline hoarder. Their old living room had bookshelves lined to the ceiling, filled with Ben's university textbooks on architecture that he'd never part with, no matter how long he'd been out of school. And globes. Ben always had a thing for globes.

Soon, their new house, with its smooth hardwood floors and many windows, would be filled with their belongings too. The place wasn't huge—more of a colonial-style home with not much space—but it was charming. Something most thirtysomethings would be grateful to afford.

"I can live with your clutter," Taylor said, "but the basement is still mine."

"I know, I know." Ben's brown eyes crinkled as he smiled, short hair tousled in a way that made him look much younger than thirty-six. "Your workspace will be spotless. Don't worry!"

Good. Taylor required a clean space to think clearly. She would have a tidy desk, a chalkboard, and one shelf containing books on psychology and serial killers, which she would read time and again to keep her mind fresh.

Ever since she was a child, Taylor had been drawn to the macabre—it sounded dark, but it made her good at her job. It was in her genes, after all; her father was a clinical psychologist with an emphasis on psychopaths. Ben only knew the surface of how deep these thoughts went. When Taylor was on a case, she would lock herself in the basement for hours reading books. Thinking. Theorizing.

And allowing her mind to descend into what it felt like to *be* a killer.

"If this isn't a hell of a view," Ben said, breaking Taylor's thoughts before she could go down a darker path.

"It's gorgeous," she agreed.

They faced the bay window, which had a breathtaking view of the ocean in the distance. The afternoon sun glistened off the waves in golden sparks as they rolled into shore.

Coastal Virginia had never been where Taylor thought she'd end up, especially a place like Pelican Beach, with its quaint boardwalk by the shore and family-owned gift shops. But maybe the change of scenery would provide a more stable life for their one-day family. Besides, Taylor's father was only a thirty-minute drive away in Baltimore. Maybe here, in this idyllic house facing the ocean, with new jobs and new friends, they would both find solace, and Taylor's urge to run would disappear forever.

"Hey," Taylor squeezed Ben's hand, smiling at him, and their eyes met. "I really am happy to be here."

"Me too. This is gonna be great for us." He squeezed her back. "And hey, let's head down to the beach later. I have a surprise planned for us."

"A surprise?"

Ben winked mischievously.

Oh God. Ben's 'surprises' typically ranged from sweet reservations at bistros to completely out of the blue, unpredictable, random, and sometimes unfavorable events.

"As long as it's not another henna tattoo parlor," Taylor muttered, and Ben chuckled.

"No promises."

They went upstairs, where three empty bedrooms waited for them. They stopped outside of the smallest room at the end of the hall.

"Maybe we'll have some little ones in here someday," Ben said.

Taylor shut her eyes and pictured baby blue walls and a crib, until—

Blood splatter on toys. A baby's mobile still turning.

She sucked in a breath and forced herself back to the present. Her heart battled her ribcage.

Ben frowned in concern, keeping his hand on the small of her back. "You okay?"

Her chest constricted as the images bombarded her. That crime scene in Portland had been particularly grisly. Kids—why did it have to be kids?

Keep it together, Sage.

Bile rose to Taylor's throat. When she'd accepted the new job in Quantico and found out she'd be moving to Pelican Beach, she'd foolishly hoped the ghosts would stop following her.

But of course they won't. They're a part of me.

I need air.

"Honey—why don't we head to the beach now?" Taylor asked stiffly. "I'm, ah, excited for your surprise," she lied.

"So soon?" Ben inquired. "I mean, I'd love to, but—"

But Taylor was already thumping down the stairs, car keys in hand. Ben's footsteps thundered behind her.

"Hey, wait up!" he called.

Taylor stormed outside, onto their small and overgrown front lawn, desperate to breathe anything but tight, claustrophobic air. As soon as the salty ocean breeze filled her lungs, the images—and the suffocating feelings that came with them—melted away.

"Taylor," Ben said in a stern tone. Clearly, she wasn't as good at hiding things as she thought.

"I'm fine." She didn't look at him, just headed straight for the driver's seat. "Let's go."

***

The smell of the water was as calming as the *whoosh* of the waves on the shore, settling Taylor's panic attack by the time they reached the beach. Now, she and Ben walked down the boardwalk, ice cream cones in hand, and passed by a beach shack that sold trinkets with people's names on them and floating devices.

Still, it unnerved her that she lost face in front of Ben. It wasn't the first time, but she wanted him to think she was strong. More than that, she didn't want him to press further, to ask questions—to become burdened with the same things she was.

Three children chased each other across the beach, their tiny feet leaving footprints in the sand. One of them crashed into a sandcastle, and their giggles erupted into the air. Taylor's heart warmed.

"You know, I've never been a beach girl," she told Ben, "but it's nice here. It's a good place to raise a family."

"Yeah. I'm glad you took the job." Ben bit into his cookie dough ice cream and squinted at the afternoon sun. "And hey, it's a win-win for me. I get to design a beautiful beachfront hotel and have a new home with my beautiful wife."

"Okay, that's enough," she joked. "When am I going to see this big surprise, anyway? Or was it just the ice cream?"

"No." Ben laughed and rubbed the back of his neck. "Truth is, I'm a little nervous to take you there. I'm not sure you're gonna like it."

"Well, I don't like the sound of that."

"Just keep an open mind, okay?"

Taylor finished her cone and dropped it in a garbage can that was painted like a seagull. Ben got three scoops, so he was still biting through his waffle cone as they made their way up the downtown strip. Taylor peeked into the window of an antique shop as Ben tossed the rest of his cone in a can, making a disgusted face like he'd had way too much sugar.

Up ahead, a wooden sign stood out on the sidewalk that read TAROT READINGS in white letters.

This better not be where Ben is taking me.

But Ben planted his feet outside of the shop and apprehensively met her gaze.

"Before you say anything, I—"

"Ben, come on," Taylor said. He knew damn well she wasn't into psychic readings or astrology or anything like that.

"I said to keep an open mind!" Ben exclaimed. "Please? Just one little reading. I want to know how our new life will turn out."

“No cards are going to know that, Ben.”

“It’s just for fun.”

Damn it. Taylor wanted to make a snide comment, like: *You know tarot is all theatrics, right?* But if it meant a lot to Ben, maybe she could just be nice and play along. After all, it was *her* new job that had brought them both here in the first place.

But Taylor was not a fan of tarot readings for a reason. The truth was, she had been to one once before, years ago in a life she didn’t care to think of much anymore. That reader, all the way back in Portland, had given her the ‘Death’ card, all before one of the worst events of her life. Taylor swallowed the memory, refusing to let it surface after all these years.

It was a coincidence by a scam artist. Nothing more.

So what are you afraid of?

Taylor ran her thumb along her locket necklace.

Maybe I should give it a try. Even just to prove it’s all bullshit.

And besides, Ben was giving her those puppy dog eyes.

“Fine, fine,” she muttered.

Ben let out an enthusiastic, “Yes!” before he grabbed her hand and pulled her inside. How had she ended up with such a happy-go-lucky guy?

The bell on the door dinged, and the smell of incense burned in the air of the small, dimly lit shop. It looked as Taylor figured it would: covered in bogus astrology symbols and all-seeing eyes. Taylor expected an old crone to emerge through the purple drapes that were embossed with golden star symbols—but a slim, dainty hand appeared and moved the fabric aside. A tall, slender, and beautiful woman came out, no older than Taylor herself.

“Good afternoon,” she said, her voice velvety smooth. A long brown braid cascaded down her loose-fitting clothes, which were also a dark purple and gold. Silver chain necklaces hung around her neck and she had inquisitive, yet wise eyes. Maybe it was the lack of proper lighting, but her irises appeared pitch black.

Both Ben and Taylor were at a loss for words—they certainly hadn’t expected someone like *this.* After an awkward moment, Ben cleared his throat. “Hello there. The sign outside said you do tarot readings?”

“I do.” A curt smile crossed her red-painted lips. “My name is Miriam Belasco—most people call me Madam Belasco, but you may call me Mim, should it suit you more.”

"Hi, Mim...," Taylor trailed off. As beautiful as this woman was, she was completely strange. She gave off an elusive, mysterious energy, like a Sage in the night.

Due to Taylor's work, she couldn't help but read people when she met them; it was second nature. But Madam Belasco was unreadable. Was she the type of person to hold doors for someone? Taylor had no idea. Was she glass half full or half empty? No clue.

Surely, it was part of her act—*scam, more like*—to present herself this way. Everyone knew fortune tellers and those alike were after one thing: people's money.

But if it made Ben happy, Taylor was willing to play along—for now.

"Shall we get started?" Madam Belasco asked.

Taylor and Ben found themselves in the back of the shop, seated across from Madam Belasco at a small round table, candles lit all around them. A warm glow emanated from the flames, reflecting off the crystal ball off to the side. Even stranger, a Sage skull was placed deliberately to face them, and its black eyeholes kept distracting Taylor as Madam Belasco shuffled her cards.

"Have either of you had a reading before?" she inquired.

Taylor's jaw tightened. Ben waited for her to reply, then went first. "Yes! I have, many times."

"That's great!" Belasco said. "And you, Mrs. Sage?"

"No," Taylor peeped. Discomfort radiated up her arms. *This was a bad idea.*

"Riveting!" Belasco exclaimed. "I'm always thrilled to introduce a newcomer to the world of tarot. Might I ask your names?"

"Taylor Sage and Ben Chambers," Ben said. Taylor had kept her original last name when they married. It wasn't that she didn't like Ben's, but her father never had any sons, and she wanted the Sage name to continue with her. "But we're married," Ben added.

Madam Belasco grinned at Ben before her eyes skated over Taylor. "I sense hesitancy from you, Mrs. Sage. Your husband's reading might help ease your mind."

"Sure," Taylor muttered.

"Now," Madam Belasco turned to Ben with a warm smile that Taylor did not trust. "Would you like to ask the cards a question, or shall this be a general reading?"

"Hmm. Well, I don't want to give away too much, but I just made a big life decision. I want to know: what will this decision bring?"

Of course, Taylor knew he was referring to the move, but there was no way Belasco could. Madam Belasco shut her eyes as she shuffled the cards again before she handed them to Ben and asked him to shuffle. Then, she asked him to place the deck on the table, where she separated them into three piles. She revealed the bottom card of the first deck and flipped it up.

"How enthralling," Belasco said. "You got The Star, facing upright, for your past card. This means hope and rejuvenation. That is a great sign for your big decision, Mr. Chambers: I'm sure it means you were excited to make it. Next, we see The Hanged Man, upright, for your present. This typically means sacrifice, or martyrdom. I take it you had to sacrifice something for this new decision?"

Ben nodded. "In a way, yes… but it was a happy sacrifice."

Taylor gave him a tight-lipped smile. She knew how much he loved their old house.

"And finally…," Belasco trailed off, her warm demeanor shifting to a slightly colder one. "We have The Lovers, reversed, for your future. This means a loss of balance. Or perhaps one-sidedness."

Taylor couldn't help but feel annoyed at Ben's silence. Surely he couldn't be thinking this meant anything to do with her? Of course, there was also a tinge of guilt, because there *were* things she hid from her husband.

"What does this mean overall?" Ben asked.

Belasco's eyes crinkled as she smiled. "My interpretation is that there is much hope for your future, and you have sacrificed much to get where you are already. Unfortunately, the cards seem to believe there may be a readjustment period that may not be the easiest of times. That said, this is by no means a negative reading, Mr. Chambers. You have a bright future, but you may have more fighting and sacrificing to get there."

Ben laughed bashfully. "Well, that's good news then! I'm a fighter—whatever it is, I'll get through it!"

Taylor resisted a biting comment: *You don't really believe this, do you?*

Then, the moment Taylor was dreading: her turn.

"I don't need a specific question," she said. "General is fine."

"Very well," said Belasco.

They repeated the same process of shuffling the cards and dividing them into three decks.

“First,” Madam Belasco said, “for your past, we have The Six of Cups, reversed. This means independence, moving forward, or leaving home. Something tells me your field of work requires this.”

“You can say that again,” Ben mumbled, only to receive a glare from Taylor. He shrugged innocently, and the reading continued.

“Next, we have The Four of Pentacles, upright, for your present. This means conservation, security. Could this have anything to do with your current situation?”

Taylor didn’t reply. These cards could be attached to anything and just ‘make sense.’

“And finally, for your future, we have…,” Madam Belasco’s eyes shone in the flames, and she looked up at Taylor with the utmost seriousness. “Oh, my. I’m very sorry to say this, Mrs. Sage, but your future card reads…”

She flipped up a card featuring a grim reaper.

Taylor’s stomach twisted as Madam Belasco read out the name:

“Death.”

CHAPTER TWO

A scoff escaped Taylor's lips. This woman couldn't be serious.

But Madam Belasco stared up at her through her thick, dark lashes, like even she believed her own bullshit. "The cards aren't saying death is coming directly for you, Mrs. Sage. But it is in your future. Your near future, in fact."

Ben let out a slight gasp. "Honey, maybe we should listen."

"I'm sure I'll be fine," Taylor muttered, annoyance flushing through her. She didn't need Belasco freaking Ben out for no reason. "Look, Mim? No offense, but please don't scare my husband with these games. We just moved here, we're starting a new life together, and frankly this isn't funny."

"I understand your hesitancy," Belasco intertwined her heavily ringed fingers on the table. "But this is not a mere dramatic reading, and I assure you this is no game. I am getting a dark aura from these cards. You may be summoned sooner than you think."

"Summoned?" Taylor cocked an eyebrow.

Madam Belasco closed her eyes and laid her hands flat on the table, brows stitched, before she began shaking. Taylor shot Ben a look that said *This shit, really?* But Ben watched intently, awestruck. *Damn it.* The last thing Taylor needed was her husband keeping her up at night with nightmares over this.

"I see a girl." Belasco's voice tremored. "Oh—she's smiling! No, it's blood, so much blood…"

"All right, this is getting ridiculous." Taylor's chair skid against the floor as she stood. "Ben, we're leaving."

"Taylor, wait—"

But Taylor had already exited through the curtain to the lobby of the store. Goosebumps rose on her arms, and she rubbed them out. She knew it was all theatrical garbage, but the way Belasco spoke still freaked her out. Honestly, she didn't get why these people didn't just go into acting; their performances could be damn convincing.

Ben came out, looking sweaty and frazzled, followed by Madam Belasco, who appeared as calm as a ventriloquist doll.

Taylor stuffed her hands in the pockets of her shorts. "Do you take cash only, or is credit fine?"

Belasco took her place behind the cash register at the front desk. Her eyes glided over Taylor, making her skin crawl, before she said: "No payment is necessary. I only ask that you think about what the cards said today."

Dumbfounded, Taylor didn't reply. Psychics, fortune tellers, et cetera, were all scam artists—so why wasn't Belasco charging?

Ben insisted: "Please, let us pay."

But Belasco merely disappeared behind the curtain.

Taylor was quick to leave, Ben behind her. Relief ran through her as she exited the dank shop, onto the warm street, happy to be away from the smell of incense irritating her nostrils.

"Don't you think that was a bit rude?" Ben said. They faced each other on the sidewalk, the early afternoon sun beating down.

Exasperated, Taylor threw her arms up. "I'm sorry if I embarrassed you, Ben, but that was too much. I don't appreciate being told I have 'death' in my future by a woman who can't see five minutes in front of her."

"Well, maybe you do."

"Don't be ridiculous. I—"

Taylor's phone vibrated from her pocket, cutting her off. She and Ben exchanged a tense look before she checked the caller ID: *Winchester.* A lump formed in Taylor's throat. *Not now.*

"Special Agent Sage," she answered.

"Sage," a gruff voice said. "This is Chief Steven Winchester. We've talked on the phone."

"Chief," Taylor said, surprised. Ben raised a brow, and she turned away as she spoke into the phone. "Of course I know you. I wasn't expecting to hear from you so soon."

"I know you're in tomorrow morning, but change of plans. A new case landed. We need you and your new partner here ASAP."

Shit.

Taylor met Ben's inquisitive stare, and guilt sank her heart. He'd been so happy that they were spending one day together, no work obligations. She sighed. "Of course, sir. I'll see you in an hour."

As soon as the call ended, Ben refused to meet her eyes. "Work so soon?" he asked, disappointment heavy in his voice.

"Yeah." She stepped closer to him and grabbed his index finger in hers. That had always been their thing. On their wedding day, as they stood at the altar, Taylor had held Ben's finger as they read their vows. "I'm sorry, honey," she added quietly.

He smiled, although the sadness was clear on his face. "It's okay. I knew what I signed up for when I married an FBI agent."

Taylor kissed her husband's cheek, wishing she could go home and fantasize about their new life a little longer—but of course, some aspects of their world would always stay the same. The chief wouldn't have called her in early if it wasn't serious.

Which could only mean someone was dead.

An icy feeling wafted through her, like she was being watched—and she peered behind her to see Madam Belasco watching through the windows of the store. Their eyes met once before Belasco vanished behind the purple curtain.

"You may be summoned sooner than you think."

Taylor couldn't deny that it creeped her out.

But it was a coincidence. It had to be.

***

Chief Steven Winchester offered Taylor an oversized, meaty hand, which she shook firmly. Taylor had done her research on her new boss, and he was exactly as she expected: a cantankerous older man with a thick handlebar mustache and eyes haunted by the job. Taylor's own gaze was starting to look more like his in the mirror every day.

"Special Agent Sage, I wish we were meeting under a more positive light," Winchester said.

"What's going on?"

"Follow me."

The FBI headquarters in Quantico wasn't much different from Taylor's last office—the same types of sterile workers, the same tired and overworked agents milling about. While agents were paid to be professional pretenders, here at HQ, their masks could fall off and they could be themselves: hard workers with skeletons in their closets. They all had that in common.

Winchester led her toward a briefing room, but before he opened the door, he faced Taylor and said, "Don't let his looks fool you. He's an experienced agent and a fresh talent."

"Who?" Taylor said, but Winchester had already opened the door to reveal a small room. A man wearing a crisp navy suit turned to face them.

Taylor knew she'd be assigned a new partner—but she didn't expect this.

A fresh-faced guy who couldn't be much older than his late twenties looked at her like an excited puppy dog the moment she walked in. He jumped forward, but quickly regained his composure, probably realizing he was out of line.

"Special Agent Taylor Sage," Winchester said, "meet your new partner, Agent Calvin Scott."

Taylor extended her hand. "Great to meet you."

Calvin looked at it for a moment, dumbfounded, before he gave her an overeager shake. "Likewise," he replied a little too quickly.

Taylor couldn't help but raise an eyebrow at her new partner. Calvin was the type of guy who looked like he never left high school—clean shaven and baby faced, yet handsome in a 'cute' way. Nothing like her previous partner in Portland, Agent Jenkins, who'd been a haggard alcoholic who smoked a pack a day.

"You two can get to know each other on the drive," Winchester said, going over to a whiteboard that was turned around. "Let's keep this briefing quick."

"Drive?" Taylor asked.

She and Calvin exchanged a confused look—clearly, he was still in the dark too.

Winchester flipped the board to reveal several photographs taped to it. Taylor's nose crinkled; she'd always had a weird sensation of blood in her nose when she looked at photos of a dead body, like she could smell the crime scene without even being there. And this one was particularly gruesome.

Sickened—but oddly fascinated—Taylor stepped closer to observe the photos. One half of the board contained photos of a young man in a red dress, his head tilted back to reveal a face smeared with red lipstick and a taped-back smile like it was a prop on the set of a damn *Joker* movie. The other photos showed a similar scene, only the dress was purple, and there was no forced smile or lipstick on the face of the victim.

Taylor's skin crawled. Belasco's words from earlier resurfaced. *"I see a girl. Oh—she's smiling! No, it's blood, so much blood..."*

This was a he, not a she—yet the body was dressed as a girl…

What kind of sick joke is this? How did she know?

Taylor couldn't believe she was even entertaining the idea that the ridiculous fortune teller 'saw' something. It was a coincidence.

Either that, or Miriam Belasco was a murderer.

Won't hurt to add her to the suspect list, Taylor thought, still unnerved by the entire experience.

Winchester's voice broke into her reverie.

"The left was found this morning. Our guy on the right was last year. In two different towns, but each about forty minutes north of here."

"So it's the same killer," Calvin said.

"Maybe. Or a copycat, or not linked at all. The issue is that we have two similar crimes, in two similar locations, but they aren't exactly the same."

Taylor stepped closer to quietly study the photos. The dresses were different—Victim One in something Taylor's late grandmother might have worn, Victim Two in a high school girl's prom gown. But it was more than that. Both pictures contained two objectively similar scenes, and yet something felt eerily off about them.

Victim One looked dirty. Filthy, in fact, like a homeless person who had been shoved into a dress. Victim Two looked like his body had been scrubbed clean before he was carefully clothed, the same way a mortician might prepare a corpse for viewing. Aside from the lipstick smeared across his face, he looked like a porcelain doll.

"The first crime was messy," Taylor said without meaning to, eyes still trained on Victim One.

"The killer could be escalating," Calvin added in. "Y'know how they always start small and work their way up. Killing small animals as children, hurting other kids on the schoolyard… besides, it's common for killers to mess up the first time…"

Calvin's voice tuned out as Taylor's vision zeroed in on the photos. The rest of the world melted away. She trailed down the neckline, the torso, arms, and finally: the hands.

Victim One had dirt under his fingernails. Victim Two's had not a visible speck. But also…

Victim One had a cheap-looking ring on his index finger.

But Victim Two had a tan line on the third finger of his left hand.

Taylor's heartbeat increased the same way it always did when she found a potential clue.

"Were either of the victims married?" she asked Winchester, cutting into what Calvin was saying.

“Engaged,” Winchester said. “Red Dress was, anyway. Our purple dress man, well, we still don’t know much about him. But Red Dress was freshly engaged to his high school sweetheart.”

“So where’s his engagement ring?”

In one smooth stride, Winchester was in front of the photo, face wrinkled as he took a closer look. “Well, would you look at that. Good eye, Sage. I see your reputation wasn’t bullshit.”

Calvin peered at the photos again as well. “Damn, you’re right. I didn’t see that.”

Taylor hadn’t meant to show off. She shyly nodded. She always looked for the smallest details.

The question now was: was the ring removed post-mortem, or did he remove it himself? Taylor had an inkling it was the latter, considering Victim One still had a ring on, albeit not a wedding ring… but she needed to know more about Victim Two before drawing any conclusions.

After all, victims always reveal something about their killers.

“Well, keep at it,” Winchester said. “What little we know about the first victim is in here.” He handed a thin manila folder to Taylor. She resisted the urge to flip it open right away, since Winchester was still speaking. “We haven’t done a full examination on the new crime yet. Everything else is in this folder. I’ve requested that our red dress scene not be disturbed until you two can arrive and assess the situation live.”

“Wait,” Taylor said, “the body is still there?”

“Yes, which means that poor sonuvabitch is out there rotting in the sun, and you two need to get your asses in gear.”

“Now?” Calvin stammered, but Taylor was already at the door. This was her calling. What she was made to do.

As dark as it was, nothing both disturbed and excited her more than seeing a crime scene for the first time.

“You heard the man, Scott,” Taylor said. “Hurry up—you’re driving.”

CHAPTER THREE

Taylor chewed on her lip as she flipped through the case file in the passenger seat of Calvin Scott's car, her new partner babbling from behind the wheel.

"You were stationed in Portland before, right?" Calvin asked. "You know, I've never actually been. Does it rain as much as they say it does?"

"Yeah," Taylor muttered.

She thought back to the many dark dreary drives she'd had with Agent Jenkins back in Oregon. On one of their last cases before the move, they drove across the state during a lightning storm to observe the body of a teenage girl who had been the final victim of a state-wide serial killer. This was also the kill that finally led them to a break in the case—a piece of DNA left behind.

Jenkins never wanted to talk unless it was about the case. And so, their conversations were always meaningful. But Calvin couldn't get enough talking in.

"Yeah to Portland, or yeah to rain?"

"Both. But you already knew I was from Portland, didn't you?" She finally met his curious gaze, and he refocused on the road. "You seem to know a lot about me, and yet I know next to nothing about you. Why is that?"

Calvin rubbed the back of his neck with one hand, the other white-knuckled on the wheel. "You caught me. Truth is, I sort of already knew who you are. I heard about your work in Oregon, about the case with the mom, and the—"

Taylor gripped the folder a little too hard, crinkling it. Calvin paused, likely realizing he'd struck a nerve. A case like that would be hard on anyone.

"The mother who killed her children and tried to frame the husband," Taylor finished for him. "Yes, I was on that case."

"How did you figure out it was her? The entire media was on her side. Hell, I bought it too, really thought the husband was the bad guy."

Taylor caught a glimpse of herself in the mirror. Her long black hair tied back in a low ponytail, bangs across her forehead, steely gray eyes.

She'd never had an "innocent" look. But she'd known many women who did, and who used it to their advantage.

"No one wants to believe the young, beautiful, doe-eyed mother could be a psychopath," Taylor said. "It's a term commonly associated with white male serial killers or 'boogeymen,' and people hate having their preconceived notions flipped upside down. But the girl didn't expect to be interrogated by my partner and me as much as she was. Plus, the crime scene was too perfect—if her husband really did it, he wanted to get caught. Holes in her story started emerging. We eventually uncovered the husband had been cheating, the wife found out and wanted him to pay, so she framed him. Under pressure, she confessed. Case closed."

Taylor made it sound so simple, and yet the images from that particular crime scene haunted her to this day. She couldn't allow Calvin to see through the cracks in her veneer, though—she'd already lost herself in front of Ben earlier that day, and she wouldn't allow it to happen in a professional setting.

"Wow," Calvin said. "So what do you make of what we have now? Think it's a serial killer?"

She didn't reply. Rather, she gazed out at the rolling hills in the distance, topped by clusters of forestry native to Northern Virginia. She then turned back to the file to re-read the information.

The previous victim, Frank Turner, had been a drifter. Mid-twenties. Barely anyone knew him. Apparently, he used to frequent a local dive bar. Toxicology reports said roofies were found in his system, so the detectives on the case inferred he had been drugged at said dive bar. However, it never went anywhere, and another victim never showed up in the area.

Until now, forty minutes away from that town, with this new body found. It was close enough to be connected, but far enough to suggest the killer may not have lived there.

So who was this new victim? Taylor itched to know more. She hadn't vocalized it yet, but she was quickly building a profile of the killer based off the file: male, late twenties to early thirties, because that is when most serial killers start. Likely Caucasian due to the demographics in the area. Sexual orientation: questionable, but the obsession with dressing men in women's clothes may have been a hint.

One of the most thrilling aspects of her job was always uncovering the psyche of a new killer. With every man—or woman—she booked, she always visited those who would give her the time in prison. Most of them would. Generally, a killer's personality would do a complete shift once they were already behind bars, as they'd lose all hope of proving themselves innocent. Therefore, they could be comfortable in their own skin—displaying no empathy, being amused by the idea of hurting others. Taylor swore some of them were even relieved to finally be caught, as though a weight had been lifted and they no longer needed to *pretend.*

In a way, she understood that herself. Pretending was exhausting. Even the parts of her past she hid from Ben ate at her every day. But unlike the criminals she'd dealt with throughout her career, Taylor didn't feel the need to kill—she couldn't understand that at all. But with every evil man she hunted, she felt she was getting one step closer to truly understanding the psychopath.

***

Taylor stepped onto the pathway that snaked through Ames Park, along the shoreline of a lake glistening in the summer sun. Lake Vernon was even smaller than Pelican Beach, and it felt less touristy and more homey, with its gable-front homes and plethora of playgrounds built throughout. If Ben had seen this place, he probably would've wanted to move here instead—it felt even more family-friendly. But Taylor knew from experience that quiet towns like this often harbored the darkest secrets.

Cop cars littered the parking lot before the entrance, and two portly, smalltown cops barricaded the pathway. Taylor and Calvin flashed their FBI badges as they passed, and the cops promptly moved aside.

"Is the witness still here?" Taylor asked one of the officers.

"Yeah, guy's real shaken up."

"I'd like to have a word with him."

"Right this way."

The officer led them to a tall, lean, but innocent-looking enough man who shivered from his position on the back of a police car. His hands jittered as he took a sip of coffee, even though it was a sweltering hot summer day. When Taylor and Calvin approached, he jolted upright.

"Good afternoon," Taylor said. "We're with the FBI."

"H-hello." His voice trembled. The guy was mid-forties, athletic, and had barely a five o'clock shadow on his angular jaw.

"You're the one who found the body?"

Grimly, he nodded. "Uh, yeah, my name's Chris. Chris Levine. I've been out here since six a.m."

"Six a.m.?" Calvin's brows raised. "They ought to have let you go home by now, Chris."

"They offered, but when they said the FBI was coming, I wanted to stick around. Help out as much as possible."

"Thank you for doing that, Chris," Taylor said. "Why don't you tell us about your experience? What were you doing out this morning?"

"I was just on a jog. I saw the girl—or, the man—sitting upright on the bench, and I thought she was just asleep. But I kept running for about an hour, and when I came back, she—sorry, *he*—was still there. I wanted to help, so I touched the shoulder, and that's when the hat fell off. I didn't even realize he was a man… or that he was dead."

"That must've been hard," Taylor said. "I'm sorry you went through that."

She stayed quiet, letting Calvin pick up the next question. "And what happened after that? Did you call the police right away?"

"I'd dropped my phone because I was so startled, but yes, I called the police and I've been here since." His eyes flicked between the two agents, nervous.

"And you mentioned a straw hat," Taylor said. "What position was it in before it fell off?"

Chris said nothing, thinking, so Calvin added on: "Was it straight? Tilted?"

"Or was it hiding the face?" Taylor asked. "Because you mentioned you couldn't discern the gender."

"Now that you mention it, it was angled down," Chris said. "I couldn't see the face at all, which is why I was so shocked when I saw, you know… the smile."

Taylor nodded, exchanging a look with Calvin. She made a mental note: *why go through the trouble of taping back the smile if you're going to hide the face?*

"You don't think this could happen again, right?" Chris stammered. "I have kids… I thought this was a safe town."

Taylor forced a smile, hoping to help ease his anxiety. "Don't worry, Chris. We'll get to the bottom of this. You'll hear from us again if we have any more questions."

With that, Taylor and Calvin left the witness and continued through the park, toward where the rest of the police were clustered—and likely where the body was.

“Wonder how long it’s been since they’ve seen something like this,” Taylor muttered as they walked along the path, hands stuffed in the pockets of her slacks. “The officers look pretty shaken-up too.”

Calvin was quiet. Taylor glanced at him in her peripherals. Sweat beaded on his forehead, and she wondered if it was just the sun warming his suit or if he was nervous about what they were about to see. Winchester had said Calvin was an experienced agent, and Taylor had seen her share of bodies by the time she was his age—but some agents, even the best, could never fully turn off their emotions. She had her bad days, too, but hoped her new partner could stomach it.

When Taylor and Calvin approached the swarm of officers, a rugged man, who must have been pushing his late sixties, approached. A tuft of white hair grew from his chin, and his gold sheriff’s badge gleamed in the light.

“Good afternoon,” he said with a tip of his hat.

Taylor showed her badge. Calvin followed suit, mirroring her move.

The sheriff quickly glanced them over before he said, “I’m Sherriff Wise. Thanks for coming out.”

“Sheriff,” Taylor nodded, tucking her hands over her pants. “I’m Special Agent Taylor Sage, and this is my partner, Agent Calvin Scott. I heard you have a body.”

“Yes, ma’am. Follow me.”

Shortly up the path, behind a barricade of caution tape, the body emerged. The red dress from the photo was unmistakable. Next to it on the bench was the straw hat that must have fallen off.

Then, the smell. Metallic and putrid. Yes, that was definitely flesh in its first stages of decay. Taylor and Calvin exchanged a knowing look before they both crossed the caution tape and got a closer look at the scene.

Calvin stood back while Taylor leaned in. The victim was a young man, no older than twenty-one, and his face was clean-shaven, yet his legs and arms still had regular amounts of hair for a young man. The taped-back smile had been expertly done, with plenty of masking tape hooked to the inside of the victim’s teeth and the back of his ears.

And there was not a drop of blood. Like in the photo, only lipstick smeared all over the man’s face, and the rest of him was clean—too clean.

But when she leaned in to take a closer look, her eyes picked up on details the photo didn’t display.

Not *perfectly* clean.

Between the lipstick, underneath the tape, red dots speckled the victim's jaw.

Calvin appeared beside her. "I wonder why the dress and lipstick on a male victim?"

Taylor ignored him, stating, "Look at this—razor burn. Either he went through his entire day like that, or the killer shaved him post-mortem." She pulled the file on the last victim from her side-pack and checked the autopsy report. "The cause of death on the last victim was a single stab wound to the chest. Blood patterns suggested he was dressed post-mortem." She tucked the file away and took a closer look at the new victim. No cause of death was clear, but beneath the dress, there could have been a stab wound. Taylor wouldn't touch the scene until forensics were done, even though the urge to examine itched at her. "But look at the dress... there's not a speck on it. My gut says this victim was dressed post-mortem too."

Taylor met Calvin's eyes. He appeared to be handling everything fine. *Let's see what you're made of, Scott.*

"What do you think?" she asked. "Tell me your first theory."

"Well," Calvin began, a bit baffled, "I'd guess it's some sort of fascination with women. Or at least, women's clothes."

"The clothing part is obvious," Taylor said, "however, I'm not so sure it's about feminizing as much as it is emasculating. No... it's a mockery. The smeared lipstick, the forced smile, the feet shoved into shoes way too small. And look at the victim's arms—his physique. He's athletic."

"So you think he may have been an alpha male type? This was some sort of power play against a strong man?"

"I think it's about domination. Humiliation. But there's more than that." She paused, eyes skating over the scene. "I think he's mocking women."

Something about this crime felt personal. Taylor couldn't explain it—this was one of her 'gut feelings,' which she didn't normally delve into without tangible evidence for fear of sounding unhinged. But Taylor did have a strong intuition, and sometimes, it was right. Proving it was the hard part.

She looked around at the park. In front of the bench was the lake. Some docks up ahead. The killer could have boated in. But then again, behind them was a small forest that separated the town and the park, making it feel more private. He could have snuck in through there on foot, concealed by the night.

Taylor shut her eyes. Built up the scene in her mind.

The adrenaline from the kill is still high.

I'm strong enough to carry the weight of a dead man on my shoulders.

Boating in would increase the risk of being seen.

But in the forest late at night—no one can see me.

As her mind delved into these images, Taylor circled the victim's body to check out the rear side. The wig had been properly brushed and groomed, but at the tips of the hair, a tiny shred of a leaf was stuck between the fibers.

She went straight toward the forest.

"Hey, where are you going?" Calvin asked, jogging after her.

Taylor didn't reply, just kept moving. It wasn't personal—and she didn't mean to shut her new partner out—but when she got into work mode, nothing could stop her. Agent Jenkins had understood that well, and Calvin would get it eventually too.

They reached the edge of the forest, where a cicada buzzed and the strong smell of the trees invaded Taylor's nose. She peered around the tree line while Calvin followed suit, doing the same. Taylor saw nothing but leaves and weeds, dotted with tiny insects, but after a moment, Calvin came in with:

"Check it out—something was here."

Taylor joined his side. Sure enough, some broken twigs suggested someone had entered—or exited—the forest in this spot. "Good eye," she said.

He laughed, rubbed the back of his neck. "Boy Scouts came in handy for something."

Carefully, Taylor entered the forest, eyes trained on the ground. The forest floor was blanketed with roots, sticks, and leaves, blocking out most of the dirt. But as Taylor moved up the trail, she found a small clearing.

And in it was half of a footprint. An unusually *deep* footprint.

Someone could have been pressing down hard as they walked, or perhaps they were just heavyset.

Or maybe they were carrying the weight of a dead body on their back.

Kneeling down, Taylor snapped a few photos with her phone before she stood up straight, Calvin looking over her shoulder.

"You think the killer came through here?" he asked. "That could be anyone's footprint."

It could be. Someone could have been innocently hiking. Or a teenager snuck in to smoke pot away from the town's eyes.

But on the other side of this forest was the road, where the killer could have snuck up with his car, victim on his shoulder, and carried him through unseen. Somewhere along the line, the victim's "hair" got caught in a tree. The killer cleaned up the scene when he set it up on the bench, but he missed a spot, hence the leaf in the victim's hair.

"We need to explore every angle," was all Taylor said.

Once out of the forest, Taylor and Calvin approached Sheriff Wise, who had been smoking a cigarette off to the side of the crime scene.

Taylor flashed him the footprint on her phone. "We need to get this forest taped off and execute a full search. Get forensics in here. Agent Scott here will show you the exact location of this print."

The sheriff tipped his hat. "On it."

Sheriff Wise went to walk away, Calvin hesitantly behind, but Taylor stopped him. "Sheriff. Does the family know yet?"

He swallowed, remorse written on his aging face. "Yes. We live in a pretty tight-knit community over here. I know the Gregorys well. This is their son, Jacob. They're not taking the news well. We've left them to grieve at home until we know more."

"I know it's soon," Taylor said, "but I'd like to speak to them. Find out if there's a connection between this victim and another crime we're investigating."

"Of course. I'll get you their address."

With that, Sheriff Wise headed over to his cruiser, which was parked off the side of the pathway. Taylor stuffed her hands into her pockets, sweat pooling beneath her bangs, and glanced over the lake. The afternoon clouds were trapped in its surface. It was a beautiful spot—a spot many people in this town likely traveled.

One thing was for sure: the killer wanted people to see what he'd done. It was all a big production. He was probably getting off somewhere to the idea of all this attention. But the question still remained: why hide the face after going through so much effort to tape back the smile?

Taylor squinted into the sun, at the body still sitting upright on that bench. Another gut feeling twisted inside her. Whoever did this was just getting started.

CHAPTER FOUR

Taylor knocked on the front door of the Gregorys' modest, gable-front house, Calvin at her side. As she shoved her hands into her pants pockets, waiting for an answer, she couldn't shake the feeling that she was being watched.

She checked over her shoulder—across the street was a small bungalow with pink flamingos and garden gnomes on the lawn. An elderly woman peered through the curtains, only to quickly disappear behind them. In small towns like this, a police presence always drew the eyes of neighbors—especially when there was a murder. And wherever death went, Taylor followed.

The afternoon sun was shielded by the awning of the house, and a cicada buzzed over the middle-class cul-de-sac. After a moment, a fifty-something man in a golf shirt answered the door. This could only be Jacob's father, Mark Gregory; Taylor had seen a photo in his file. A look of dread crossed his features as he took in the appearance the two agents on his porch.

"Mr. Gregory?" Taylor asked. "We're with the FBI. We were hoping we could ask you a few questions about your son."

Before Mark could answer, an older woman in a long dress ran up behind him. She had the eyes of a mother who had just lost her son: bloodshot and devastated, like her world had been torn apart. This was Janis, Jacob's mother.

"What happened?" she asked, voice trembling. "Did you find out who hurt Jacob?"

"Not yet, ma'am," Calvin said. "May we come in?"

Grimly, Mark and Janis invited them into the house. Taylor's stomach churned; the air felt heavy with the weight of Jacob's death. Childhood photos hung on the striped wallpaper, showing Jacob as a child on the playground, as a brace-faced pre-teen, then again in a high school graduation gown. It was always an eerie feeling, seeing images of a victim when they were alive after already examining their dead body.

Taylor and Calvin followed the parents to the living room, which felt like a time warp to the '70s with its floral couches and off-white carpet. On a console table, a proud photo of Jacob was framed—his graduation from Stanford Law.

Already, Taylor found no similarities between Jacob Gregory and Frank Turner. A beloved Stanford graduate versus a homeless drifter—it made no sense. She needed to know more.

Janis's arms jittered, purple veins clear through her pale skin. Mark placed a hand on her, calming her down, then met Taylor's gaze with apprehensive eyes. He gestured to the couch opposite the loveseat, divided by a glass-topped coffee table. Taylor and Calvin sat down across from the parents. A moment of awkward silence filled the air before Taylor began with:

"First of all, I'm so sorry for your loss, Mr. and Mrs. Gregory."

They nodded, sniffling.

"I'm sure you were already informed of the way Jacob was found this morning. We don't have to relive those details, but—"

"What I want to know is why my son was found dead in a dress," Mark said. His eyes were bleary with tears, but the resentment in his voice was clear. "Not only did they murder him, but to make a mockery of him like that..."

Taylor paused, took a moment to take in Mark's reaction. Personally, she found the murder itself more disturbing than the dress—but everyone grieved in different ways. Perhaps it was easier for Mark to focus on the dress.

"Unfortunately, we aren't sure why Jacob was wearing the dress," Taylor said, "but we do intend to find out." From her side bag, Taylor pulled out the file on Jacob Gregory and skimmed the pages. She'd already studied on the car ride here, but had to make sure she got everything right. "I understand that Jacob lived in D.C., yes? And he worked at a law firm."

Janis inhaled a shaky breath before she snapped, "It's in the file, isn't it? We already talked to police earlier."

Taylor's stomach sank. Talking to grieving parents never got any easier. Sometimes they screamed, cried, or directed their emotions at her. Taylor couldn't pretend to fully understand what they were going through, but the whole situation—seeing parents mourn their lost children—did hit a little too close to home for her.

Thankfully, Calvin took over. With a gentle voice, he said, "We understand how frustrating this must be. We're just trying to understand everything we can about Jacob so we can find out who did this to him."

After a moment, Janis nodded. "Ask whatever you need to."

The tension in the room only grew more palpable, but Taylor didn't have time to hesitate.

"If Jacob lived in D.C., what was he doing here?" she asked. "We understand he had a fiancé. Did she not join him?"

"Jake comes to visit us on weekends sometimes," Mark said. "Marcy—his fiancé—normally can't make it. She works nights, so... Jake likes to come home whenever he can."

"But what does Jacob do when he comes home, in general?" Taylor asked.

"He goes out sometimes with his childhood friends, sometimes to the bars, I think, but he always comes back."

"Not last night, though," Taylor said. "That didn't strike you as odd?"

"Of course it was odd," Mark said, "but he's our son, and he's twenty-six years old—we don't keep a leash on him!"

More silence. Janis covered her mouth with her hand as she stifled tears, and Mark looked away, shame written on his face.

Uncomfortably, Taylor uncrossed and recrossed her legs, her professional work attire—slacks and a blouse—ever-hot. "I apologize if I offended you."

Mark huffed. Gathered himself. Then, "No, I'm sorry. This whole thing has been a nightmare. I know you're just doing your job." He took a deep breath. "It *did* strike me as odd that Jacob didn't come home last night, and he didn't answer my phone call, but... I just passed it off, assumed he was drinking with his buddies." His eyes watered, and he wiped them away with his bare wrists. "Maybe if I'd gone and looked for him, he—"

"You can't blame yourself," Calvin cut in.

Taylor fidgeted with her wedding ring, pondering this information.

Visits home without his fiancé. A missing engagement ring. Late nights out.

She still saw no connection between Jacob Gregory and Frank Turner—but that didn't mean there wasn't one. And as it always was, there was a high chance Jacob's parents didn't know *everything* about their son.

Taylor faced the parents again. "Do you mind if I take a look at the room Jacob was staying in?"

Mark brought Taylor upstairs, leaving Calvin with Janis. Taylor found herself on the upper level, where the sunlight poured in through the widows, creating golden squares on the hardwood floors. Being upstairs in a stranger's home always felt too intimate. Even more so, rifling through someone's bedroom.

At the end of the hall, Mark opened a door to a small bedroom. The bed was neat, the dark blue sheets untouched. Old football trophies collected dust on the dresser. This must have been Jacob's room growing up, too; there were still pinholes in the drywall from where his old posters were hung up.

"Take your time," Mark mumbled without looking in the room, then sulked down the stairs.

A breath, and Taylor made her way through the room. A few shirts were hung up in the closet, and a suitcase sat half-open beside the bed. Taylor opened up the drawers—most were empty, save for a few old socks or pairs of pants Jacob's parents clearly never bothered to throw away.

But when she reached the bottom drawer, it rattled as she opened it. Inside was a toy car, red with a flame stripe—a relic from Jacob's childhood.

Taylor felt sick. Just as she was closing the drawer, ready to move on, something else jostled inside. She looked back in.

Along the edge of the drawer, the liner had shifted out of place.

Taylor paused. Then, using her fingernail, she peeled up the liner, slowly, until it was entirely off.

Her heart shifted in her chest.

Underneath the liner was a credit card, face-up. And judging by the shiny plastic, it had barely been used.

Taylor's mind raced. The ring, the nights home, and now this: the secret credit card. Maybe Jacob was buying things he shouldn't have been: drugs, porn, maybe even a gun. Or maybe it was simpler: he was seeing another woman, and this credit card would be filled with evidence of their dates.

Either way, Jacob Gregory was hiding something—and Taylor intended to find out what.

***

With the credit card face-up on the table, Taylor scrolled through her laptop at the Quantico headquarters. On her screen was the history of Jacob's apparent secret card. She knew it was part of her job, but going through a man's dirty laundry never felt like a clean task.

But this time was different. She'd gone through many credit cards of both victims and suspects—she'd seen everything from kink porn to even more illegal, disturbing findings. Jacob, however, only ever seemed to use this card at one place, about once every one to two months.

Jackhammer.

And it went back for nearly six years.

If Taylor had to guess—she'd assume it was a bar or a strip club. But why have a secret card just for that?

Just as she was about to dive deeper, the door opened and Calvin entered with, "Forensics are in."

Taylor faced him in the swivel chair, and Calvin pulled one up to position himself across the table from her. He spread the papers out, and Taylor eagerly grabbed them, reading as fast as her eyes would allow.

No blood was found at the scene—not the victim's or otherwise. Not a speck of DNA belonging to anyone but the victim.

The footprint in the forest brought back no matches—it was only a partial, and seemed generic. The police had scoured the forest, but found no other visible tracks or anything that might identify the killer. There was also no evidence of Jacob ever being through there.

As for the body—the cause of death was, indeed, a single stab wound to the chest.

Which meant the same man who killed Frank Turner last year had to be the same guy who killed Jacob Gregory last night.

"What do you think it means?" Calvin asked.

Taylor pondered for a moment, tapping her nails against the table. She didn't want to jump to conclusions—but the story building around Jacob Gregory and the circumstances of his death were starting to become clear.

"I think it means we're dealing with the same killer," Taylor said. "What'd you find on Jacob's social media?"

"Not much. The guy had tons of friends, and from what I can tell, was caring and loyal to his fiancé. Even his private messages are squeaky clean—he never so much as flirted with another woman. His conversations were always friendly and supportive. No secrets there."

Taylor turned the laptop to him and leaned over the table so they could both see. She scrolled down, allowing Calvin to take in the list of purchases. He frowned, thinking on it, and Taylor took out her phone, searching *Jackhammer.*

One result came up nearby. About an hour away, in a town called Kinallen.

Taylor paused, re-read a couple of times to ensure she understood.

Most of the cases she'd dealt with in her career involved exposing someone in one way or another—but usually, it was the killer whose secret life she had to dig up.

But the description of the bar read: *LGBTQ bar with a classic feel,* and on the reviews, all customers were saying it was almost exclusively gay men who attended.

Morally, Taylor didn't want to disclose this. But it was her job to find out who killed Jacob Gregory, by any means necessary—so she had no choice. Being an agent often involved putting one's own morals aside for the greater good.

"It appears to be a gay bar," Taylor said.

Calvin leaned back in his chair, crossed his hands behind his neck. "Why get engaged, then? Was he gonna call it off, or just lead a bisexual life?"

Taylor slid her wedding ring up her finger, then down again. Mark did seem particularly disturbed that Jacob was found in a dress—there could be homophobia in the family. Maybe Jacob was ashamed of who he really was, and felt the need to hide it behind his fiancé and seemingly perfect life in D.C.

The only person who could truly answer those questions was Jacob himself. All Taylor knew for sure was: Jacob Gregory was living a double life.

Maybe that was what got him killed.

Taylor shut the laptop and stood, slinging her work bag over her shoulder. "Should we go for a drink?"

CHAPTER FIVE

As Taylor entered Jackhammer, the masculine scent of cologne swallowed her. It was only six p.m., and the tables were sparsely occupied by young to middle-aged customers. Eighties music played from the jukebox as Taylor and Calvin crossed to the neon sign that read BAR. It was small place, more like a dive bar than a nightclub, but the multihued lights made it feel trendy and alive.

She glanced around the room as she crossed. The stools Jacob probably sat on. The pinball machine he may have played. The faces of the patrons, curiously glancing her way—men who may have known him. Jacob had been coming here for years, and somehow, not a single person who knew him found out. It was a lot to commit to; she could only imagine how much that secret weighed on him.

As Taylor reached the bar, the bartender—an attractive, tattooed man—looked at her like he didn't know where the hell she came from. As she'd read online, it was clearly rare to see a woman here. He dried off a cup with a rag, and Taylor took the liberty to flash her badge, along with Calvin. The bartender's face went pale beneath his large beard.

"Did someone get hurt?" he asked.

Taylor studied him. He seemed nice enough, but if he was jumping straight to violence, she couldn't help but sense he had a deeper reason. How often did people get in fights at this bar?

"Why would you think that?" she asked.

"Ah, sorry," he said. "Police always make a bartender nervous. I deal with a lot of rowdy folks. What can I help you with?"

Taking out her phone, Taylor opened up a photo of Jacob and showed the bartender. "Do you recognize this man?"

The bartender observed the photo. Recognition crossed his gruff features, and still, he had nervous eyes. He nodded and said, "Yeah, I know him. He comes here a lot, has for a few years, but I haven't seen him in over a month."

And the card had been hidden last night. Which means Jacob didn't plan on coming here the night he was killed...

"Any ideas why he may have stopped coming?" Taylor asked.

He put away the cup he was drying. "Actually, there is." He glanced around the bar—no customers nearby, but he still lowered his voice as he said, "We had an incident the last time he was here. This homophobe sometimes hangs around outside the bar and harasses my patrons. Normally, people just ignore him, but...," the bartender swallowed nervously. "I wanted to bring it to the police, but the victim—that guy in the picture, Jack I think his name is—wouldn't let me."

Jack. That must have been Jacob's alter-ego. And if he was known as Jack—maybe there was a fake ID somewhere out there to match. Taylor added that to the mental list of potential clues to find.

"What happened with Jack?" Taylor pressed, choosing not to correct the name.

"That asshole was calling him a whole slew of names I won't dare to repeat," the bartender continued. "Then I guess Jack tried to ignore him, only to get a bottle thrown at his head. He was banged up pretty good, but refused to go to the hospital. I helped him out, tended to his wounds in the back, then he disappeared. I haven't seen him since."

"And do you have an exact date this event occurred?" Calvin asked.

"Uh, sometime early June... might have been the third or fourth. Sorry, I can't remember exactly." The bartender glanced between Taylor and Calvin, looking apprehensive. "Look, no offense, but I've reported that homophobic asshole to the cops a few times and they've done nothing to stop him from harassing my customers."

"We'll be different," Taylor said. "That's a promise."

The bartender hesitantly nodded. She had no more questions for now—but something in her gut told her she'd be seeing this bar again.

"Thanks for your time," Calvin said as he and Taylor turned to leave, but the bartender stopped them.

"Hey, is Jack okay? What's this all about?"

Taylor glanced at Calvin, then said, "I'm sorry, but Jack is a victim in a homicide investigation."

A look of sadness spread across the bartender's face, his blue eyes downcast, but he said nothing.

Taylor pulled a card out from the inside of her blouse pocket and placed it on the bar. "If you think of anything else that might be useful, please give us a call."

With that, Taylor and Calvin crossed the bar, gaining more looks from customers as they did so. For now, they had their first lead.

At most, that homophobe was guilty of assault.

At worst—murder.

Either way, the next move was to track him down.

***

The loud buzz of a saw rattled Taylor's brain as she and Calvin cut through a jobsite on a lot on the east end of town. Construction workers gathered around a massive hole in the ground while others moved giant metal bars with forklifts. If Taylor had to guess, they were in the early stages of constructing a new apartment building. It was still light out, but the sun would set in a couple of hours—that didn't stop these sweaty men from digging their shovels in the dirt.

Facial recognition run on a security camera from the night the bartender had described had yielded one match: Tim Dallas, a pudgy construction worker with a criminal record of a few assaults and petty theft charges. Taylor and Calvin had gathered the information quick—it was one of the many perks of working for the FBI. Back when Taylor's career first began, and she was nothing more than a twenty-one-year-old beat cop, she had to jump through hoops to get information. But the FBI had an arsenal of resources, and accessing street cams in a matter of minutes was one of them.

Taylor could tell just by glancing around that these workers were rough types. Tattooed and scarred, they eyed Taylor and Calvin up like pieces of meat as they walked through. Taylor kept her sights forward, ignoring the looks until the men refocused on their jobs.

"What do you think?" Calvin muttered to Taylor. "Should we take Tim down to the station? We do have him assaulting Jacob on video."

Taylor nodded. "We should take him in no matter what… but be cautious. Something tells me he won't go easily."

A short, overweight, balding man stood off to the side next to a group digging a hole, wearing a bright orange reflector over denim overalls. This was definitely Tim Dallas—Taylor wouldn't forget that face, even if she'd only seen him on grainy security footage.

He crammed a sandwich in his mouth. As soon as he saw Taylor and Calvin, a sour look crossed his face.

"Are you Tim Dallas?" Taylor asked.

"Yeah, who's asking?" he replied, mouth half-full of tuna salad. The fishy smell made Taylor's gut turn. Was this slob capable of such a precise murder?

Taylor and Calvin showed their badges, and Calvin said, "We'd like to ask you a few questions."

"What the hell is this?" Tim demanded. "Can't you see I'm busy?"

"You had an altercation with a man outside of a bar called Jackhammer about a month ago," Taylor said. "Do you know what I'm referring to?"

This made his face twist in rage even more. *"That's* what this is about? That guy had it coming—you know what that Jackhammer place is, right? It's *disgusting."*

"'That guy' was Jacob Gregory," Calvin said, "and he was murdered sometime last night."

Tim's face dropped. He swallowed the last bite of his sandwich. "Well what's it got to do with me?"

As Tim wiped his hands off on his overalls, Taylor noticed more eyes on them. A few workers had put down their tools and were closing in, trying to listen to the conversation.

Taylor focused on Tim. "Where were you last night?"

"Seriously?" He had the gall to laugh, which frankly, made Taylor want to arrest him even more. Even if he didn't kill Jacob—he was still an abuser, a harasser. "I'll tell you exactly where I was last night," Tim went on. "My wife's sister's house, all day and all night, for some bullshit family gathering. And trust me, my wife's sister? She hates my guts. So there's no reason for that bitch to cover for my ass. I didn't kill anyone, haven't even thought about that nasty bar since that night."

Taylor looked for any signs of deceit, but saw nothing but an idiotic oaf. She would definitely be confirming his alibi—but as much as she hated to admit it, it seemed genuine. Tim Dallas was likely not their killer, but that didn't mean he was innocent.

"We'll look into that," Calvin said. "In the meantime, why don't you take a quick ride with us down to the station?"

"What for? I didn't do shit!" More rage contorted Tim's round face. "You wanna arrest me? For what? Go ahead and try!"

He took a step closer to Calvin, and Taylor instinctively took a defensive stance. In this line of work, she had to be ready for anything—and sometimes things could turn ugly fast. Tensions were rising quick, and her adrenaline turned on.

"You think you're cute, dressing up like a detective?" Tim spat in Calvin's face. "You look like *you* belong in that little gay bar, pretty boy."

The crowd of workers—who had now fully circled them—laughed.

Calvin didn't back down. "We have footage of you assaulting and harassing a young man who is now dead." His hand found his belt. "Now you can either come with us willingly, or we can remove you ourselves."

Shit. This wasn't what Taylor had meant by 'be cautious'—she would have merely tricked Tim into coming in for questioning, but clearly, Calvin—despite his unimposing nature—still liked to do things the hard way.

But before Taylor could step in to mediate, Tim's fist flew toward Calvin's face and clocked him in the nose. Calvin recoiled, and blood immediately spilled down his pale skin. Taylor went to jump in, but Tim was already on her—ready to throw a fist at her, too.

Taylor's instincts took over. She dodged Tim's hit and jumped behind him. He was short for a man—only inches taller than Taylor—but was way heavier. Taylor wouldn't let that stop her.

Ever since she was a kid, she never wanted her smaller size to impede her ability to defend herself. She'd trained in taekwondo, karate, and even jiujitsu—in this case, she took a lesson from her black belt course. She ducked below Tim's sight and charged his legs, hurling him to the ground in a double leg takedown. Tim fell back-first, and his head smashed off the ground as Taylor pinned herself on top of him.

Tim groaned in pain, and Taylor flipped him onto his stomach. She dug her foot into his back to keep him in place.

Silence spread across the yard. The spectating workers muttered to themselves—some gasped, some even laughed. But they all backed away as Calvin slapped cuffs on Tim. Clearly, he didn't have many allies.

"You just assaulted two federal agents," Calvin said. "Now, you have the right to remain silent. Anything you say can and will be used against you in a court of law."

As Calvin continued reading Tim his rights, Taylor lifted her foot off Tim. This pathetic, angry man didn't have the skill to pull off a murder like Jacob's—Taylor felt it in her gut.

Once they had him cuffed and standing back up on wobbly feet, Taylor took over and grabbed onto Tim, forcing him to stay still. She then took in Calvin's rough appearance. Blood was drying to his pale skin, but it had been pouring like a faucet just moments ago. Taylor couldn't have her partner walking around with a busted-up nose. She sighed.

“Scott, let me take your car and deal with this piece of shit,” she said as Tim struggled against her. “I’ll drop you off at the hospital.”

“That bad, huh?” Calvin took out his phone and checked his reflection in its screen. “Oh, boy. A quick visit wouldn’t hurt.”

“Let me go, damn it!” Tim shouted.

Taylor shoved him forward, forcing him to walk with them, out of the construction site. As pleased as she was to get another piece of shit off the streets, whoever killed Jacob Gregory was still out there. Maybe looking for his next victim.

CHAPTER SIX

Taylor shoved Tim Dallas into the doors of the Kinallen police department. Even though he was cuffed, he struggled against her, and she felt like she was hauling a chained bull.

"Let go of me!" Tim shouted, his tuna breath stinking up the vestibule. "I told you, I've got an alibi!"

Taylor wasn't about to dignify Tim with a response. Even if he wasn't their killer—he was a violent homophobe, and that was more than enough to get him on Taylor's shit list. She pushed him past the next set of doors, into the lobby of the small station. The air was hot and dank inside—fans sputtered at an underworked staff, and when the receptionist saw Taylor and Tim, she stood up with wide eyes.

Tim thrashed again, nearly escaping Taylor's grip on him. This guy would just not quit. Taylor resisted the urge to shove an elbow in his kidney just to shut him up, but saved face; she didn't need this small-town station thinking the FBI resorted to violence first. She'd always liked to think of herself as more of a peace keeper—or a peace *seeker,* anyway.

Thankfully, two young male officers swiftly came over and each took one of Tim's arms. He tried to wrestle his way out, but quickly gave up. Taylor flashed the officers her badge to confirm her identity, but she was also out of breath and exhausted from hauling this guy in.

"I told you," Tim huffed, "I've got an alibi."

"I'll be sure to check that," Taylor said.

Just then, a voice bellowed over the station: "Damn it, Dallas, what'd you do this time?"

A tall, older man with a clean-shaven face hurried over. This must have been the sheriff. His gaze flicked from Dallas to Taylor, and she put her hands in her pockets, feeling a bit uncomfortable with all these eyes on her.

"This man assaulted a federal agent," Taylor told him. "The FBI has also acquired footage of him assaulting a man who is now a homicide victim."

The sheriff's eyebrows raised, and he looked at Tim, just as Tim sputtered, "I didn't kill anyone. Check my goddamn alibi, I was at my sister-in-law's, for fuck's sake!"

"Fellas, get him in a cell," the sheriff said to the young officers, who dragged Tim away, quite literally kicking and screaming. Taylor didn't understand how he still had an ounce of energy left.

Once they were alone, Taylor and the sheriff—whose badge read Coleman—stepped off to the side of the reception desk.

"What's this all about?" Coleman asked.

"I'm investigating a murder that occurred in Vernon Lake," Taylor said. "The victim sometimes came to this town, to a bar called Jackhammer. Dallas assaulted him last month, and now the victim is dead. Long story short, Dallas here is a suspect."

"Oh, brother." The sheriff ran his hand through his short brown hair. "I've been dealing with Tim Dallas for years. The guy loves to cause trouble…"

"Right now, all we can confirm are the assaults, but we'll be looking into him."

"Well, if there's anything I can do to help, let me know. We don't see a lot of federal agents over here."

Most small towns didn't, although Taylor found herself in them more often than not. Something about tiny, tight-knit communities seemed to harbor evil, and sometimes, that evil would lash out and show its true face.

"Actually, you can help," Taylor said. "I need to talk to Dallas's sister-in-law. Do you know her?"

"Yup," he droned out, taking a card and pen from his pocket. He began jotting something down, then handed it to Taylor. The card had an address on it, along with the name Bethany Hardy. "Beth can be rough too," the sheriff said, "but she's a decent Samaritan. She won't be surprised to see you. Lord knows I've knocked on that door enough times looking for Tim."

"Right." Taylor nodded. "Thanks, Sheriff."

She went to walk away, but the sheriff said, "Tim's always been a character, but I never thought he was capable of murder. I hope you find what you're looking for." He tipped his hat and walked away.

But that had been Taylor's gut instinct as well—not that Dallas would never drunkenly murder someone, but that he wasn't capable of the precise, gruesome scene she had observed earlier that day. But there was only one way to find out. Taylor gripped the card with Tim's sister-in-law's address.

Step one: confirm the alibi.

***

Taylor knocked on the screen door of a trailer on the outskirts of town. It was dark now, and mosquitos nipped at the lamp that had been activated by her presence. The voices of a couple people, followed by some stomping, bellowed from inside. Moments later, two freckled eight-year-olds whipped open the door.

"Hi!" they exclaimed.

Taylor was stunned for a moment. She hadn't expected there to be kids here. Sometimes, seeing children—their innocent eyes and heart-warming smiles—struck a nerve for her. Mostly because she wanted kids of her own, but didn't know how—or if—it would even be possible in this line of work.

But that was why she and Ben had moved to Pelican Beach, right? To start a family. They had the extra space now and everything… but something in Taylor still resisted the idea, even though she knew Ben was expecting something to happen, and for it to happen soon. Whenever the conversation came up, she sort of just avoided it.

Just as Taylor was about to ask for their mom, a woman in a housecoat shoved her way to the door, and the kids scurried off.

"What's this about?" the woman asked. This must have been Bethany, Tim Dallas's sister-in-law.

"Sorry to bother you this late, ma'am," Taylor said. Typically, she wouldn't do interviews after dark, but every passing second meant another second the killer had to plot his next crime. So if Tim Dallas was him, Taylor needed to know. Taylor continued, "I'm with the FBI. We're investigating an incident that may involve your brother-in-law, Tim Dallas."

"Oh, brother," Bethany droned. "What'd he do this time?"

"Can you tell me if Tim was here last night?"

"Yep, that lazy son of a bitch was here all night, drunk and passed out on my couch. When I got up in the morning, he was in the same position he fell asleep in… I don't think he moved a muscle."

Damn it. Alibi checks out.

Taylor had a feeling it would, but her life would be so much easier if Tim Dallas *were* guilty. But she liked to think she had a sense for evil, and from the moment she'd laid eyes on him, Tim Dallas had seemed more stupid than sinister.

"Thanks for your time," she muttered.

"Tim in trouble?" Bethany asked, but Taylor was already walking down the broken-up pathway.

"We have him down at the station," she said over her shoulder. "The sheriff can tell you more."

Taylor didn't mean to be rude, but it was getting late, and she had more work to do before she was ready to throw in the towel. Thankfully, Bethany didn't press; she was probably used to Tim getting in shit, like everyone else in this town seemed to be. The door to the trailer closed without a fuss.

After returning to Calvin's car, Taylor drove to the outer edge of the quiet park and idled beneath a tree. It was still strange driving his car without him—it smelled like him, and even though he was a federal agent, something still felt very late-twenties about it. Probably the pop can in the backseat's cup holder he'd forgotten to throw out.

She turned off the ignition and took a moment to relax, breathing out through her nose and letting her eyes shut. It felt like the first moment she'd allowed herself to relax that day.

She checked her phone: three texts from Ben. One from Calvin.

She checked Calvin's first.

Hey, I'm alive. Should be discharged soon. Gonna need my car back, lol.

Taylor texted: **I'll be there in ten.**

Nerves grew inside her as she opened up Ben's messages, mostly because Taylor knew that no matter what he said, she was going to have to deliver bad news: she wasn't going home tonight. Not when there was still so much work to do. She loved Ben, but he would be a distraction. Ben used to be softer when it came to her work, but before they moved from Portland, he had begun to grow restless with her constant overtime. Moving here was supposed to be a bit of a break, but Taylor didn't choose to have a murder like this dropped in her lap the moment they arrived.

She just prayed Ben would understand, and be the husband she needed him to be.

The texts read:

Hey honey, when can I expect you home?

Should I eat without you?

Okay, eating now—hope you're coming home soon.

With a sigh, Taylor typed, but didn't send: **Sorry, hon, I won't make it home tonight. Working a case. Need room to think. I love you and I'll make it up to you tomorrow.**

She cringed, wishing it didn't have to be this way—it was their first night at their new home, and Ben would definitely be disappointed. Not to mention, the movers would be coming tomorrow with all their furniture and Taylor wouldn't be there to help. She and Ben had planned to drink wine and sleep on a sleeping bag together that night, and have a fun night like they were in their twenties again—or early thirties, for Ben.

Taylor had met Ben when she was twenty-eight, and he was thirty. She was out at a bar in downtown Portland in a sort of FBI academy reunion with a bunch of her former classmates. Taylor wasn't much of a drinker, partier, or socializer, but she'd wanted to catch up, to learn about the many interesting cases her former peers were now working on. At that point, Taylor, herself, was a junior agent and had been climbing the ladder for many years.

She was also not looking to date. But then, when she was at the bar ready to settle up, the bartender handed her a raspberry martini—a drink way, way sweeter than anything she'd ever choose on her own. He pointed to a handsome, brown-eyed man who sat across the bar. Normally, she'd reject such a cheesy, overdone advance—but something in his rugged, bed-headed appearance and lopsided smile made her grin, which gave him a window to slide over and talk her up.

"You got my drink wrong," she'd told him.

"Oh, crap," he'd said, running his hands through his hair nervously. "Too sweet?" When Taylor nodded, he cursed, "Damn. My second choice was a gin and tonic."

Taylor almost smirked. Something about him was cute and endearing to her, which she hadn't felt about many men. "That would've been much better." She took a sip from the tiny straw. "But a bit of sugar wouldn't hurt."

"I'm Ben, Ben Chambers," he said, offering her a hand. Taylor shook it. She liked how warm his skin felt.

"Taylor Sage."

"What brings you here, Ms. Sage?"

She glanced back at her table of former FBI academy classmates, cheering their beers, then met Ben's curious gaze. "I'm with some old friends." She paused. "We were at the FBI academy together."

Ben's eyebrows shot up. "You're an FBI agent?"

“I am,” Taylor said. She figured there was no beating around the bush. The fact that she was an agent would probably scare him off anyway, if he was just looking for an easy hookup.

Except it didn’t. Ben said, “Wow, you must be busy.”

“Too busy to date,” Taylor said.

Ben wore a playful smirk. “I’m sure the right person could work around your schedule.”

Taylor snapped out of her reverie, into the present. It had been a while since she’d reminiscence on her first encounter with Ben. But it was true, even when he was just a random person hitting on her, she told him upfront that she was an agent. They’d discussed many times how Taylor’s career always had to come first.

Although, in recent years, that hadn’t stopped him from slowly growing to resent her job. He never said it, but sometimes Taylor could just *feel* it.

But there was a killer out there. Ben knew what he signed up for when he fell for a federal agent, so she pressed ‘send’ on the text and tucked her phone away.

***

When Taylor pulled out in front of the hospital, Calvin was already there waiting, an ice pack held to his nose. Good—it wasn’t as bad as Taylor had worried. Nighttime bathed the hospital grounds, but the many street lights illuminated Calvin as he approached the vehicle and got into the passenger’s side.

“Role reversal, huh?” Calvin joked and buckled his seat belt.

Taylor resisted a smirk. After spending a whole day with him, she had to admit his subtle humor was growing on her. Plus, despite it being reckless, she did admire that Calvin was willing to stand up to Tim earlier, even when they were way outnumbered. It meant he had guts, which ignited some faith in her that he’d turn out to be a solid, reliable partner.

“Cute,” Taylor muttered sarcastically before she started up the car and began the drive through the small town. “How’s the broken nose?”

“Not broken, thankfully,” Calvin said. He adjusted the seat to accommodate his long legs. “Just bruised. And bloody.” He paused as they continued driving through the night, then said, “It’s pretty late. Think we should head back to Quantico?” He glanced at her hand as she drove. “You have a husband to get home to, right?”

"I do." Taylor pressed her lips together. "But I think it's best if we stay the night here. Mull over the case files a bit more."

"You're the boss."

After a short drive, they pulled up to the nearest motel, which was as gaudy as all the motels Taylor had stayed at during her career: a flickering neon sign, half the letters burned out, and shrubbery that hadn't seen water in ages. Taylor grabbed the first parking spot, and both she and Calvin stepped into the warm summer night.

"Wait here, I'll grab our keys," he said, then zipped inside.

Taylor hugged herself and glanced up at the stars. A ball of anxiety grew in her once she was alone. She'd been avoiding checking her phone, afraid of Ben's response, but now was the time. She pulled it out.

Ben had texted: **OK sweetheart. Good luck! Will I see you tomorrow?**

She replied: **Yes, tomorrow evening. Promise.**

But she couldn't promise that—something work-related could easily come up. Her heart sank. *I shouldn't lie to him.* Just as she was ruminating over whether this was a mistake or not, Calvin appeared with two room keys dangling from his index finger.

"We're right next to each other," he said.

"Perfect," Taylor said, "but no offense, Scott, sometimes I need to work alone."

He gave her a half smile. "No skin off my back. You let me know if you come up with anything. I'll be brainstorming and sleeping, mostly."

They followed the path to their doors across the parking lot. Taylor nodded at Calvin, and he nodded back before he disappeared into his room. Taylor unlocked her door and pushed inside. It was dark, so she flicked on the light. The smell of mothballs stagnated in the air, and she threw her laptop and bag on the bed. As an agent, she was always prepared for emergencies such as this—she didn't have her pajamas, but a spare toothbrush and face wash were in her purse.

She wasted no time. Setting up her laptop at the table, she sat down in the rickety chair, ready to continue. All that work today, and they were no closer to finding the killer. Taylor figured that if she couldn't find out what happened to Victim Two—maybe she should return to Victim One.

She pulled up Frank Turner's case file. There wasn't much there—the man grew up in foster care and aged out of the system. No family, no close friends. A few arrest records here and there, but mostly for vagrancy. Some petty theft. Nothing that would explain his murder.

Taylor tugged at her wedding ring, a habit she'd developed while thinking, ever since Ben had put the ring on her.

Frank was a drifter, but that didn't necessarily mean he didn't exist. Maybe he still had some social media presence. Taylor pulled up Facebook and typed in his name and location. A profile popped up. The picture was a selfie of a younger Frank, staring intensely into the camera—looking much different than the lifeless corpse Taylor had seen in the photo earlier. But it was definitely the same man, with gruff facial hair and milky brown eyes. He wasn't a bad looking man, and was in relatively decent shape, but he did have a drugged-out aura about him.

His profile was public. Most statuses were just ramblings—he wrote paragraphs upon paragraphs about conspiracy theories, something about reptile men and the U.S. government.

Also, the last post happened two years before he died. So getting murdered wasn't what got Frank Turner off social media.

If only Frank had someone—anyone—Taylor could talk to, then she might be able to learn more. But even his social media was lonely.

A light went off in Taylor's head. Of course, Frank had no one—but Jacob had someone very important she could interview.

And the next logical choice could only be his fiancé.

CHAPTER SEVEN

Taylor held her coffee tight in her hand as Calvin knocked on the door of Jacob's apartment, where his fiancé still lived. They'd come a long way from yesterday's small town trailer park, from the motel with the stiff bed and crusty sheets.

At the crack of dawn, Taylor had ushered Calvin on the road quick, letting him take over driving. They were in D.C. within three hours, and now stood in the posh hallway of Jacob's apartment. The apartment building smelled clean and well-taken care of, like potpourri and Lysol. Taylor couldn't help but think this was a nice life Jacob had been running from.

After a few more knocks, Marcy, Jacob's fiancé, answered the door. Tears streamed down her naturally tanned cheeks, and she wore a matching set of floral pajamas. She looked at them in shock, and discomfort immediately radiated through Taylor—she could only imagine what it would be like if Ben had been murdered, and she had agents at her door while she was still in pajamas, mourning his loss. But invading people's lives was part of Taylor's job, and for the greater good.

"Ms. Garcia?" Taylor asked, flashing her badge. "Sorry to bother you so early. Do you mind if we chat for a few moments?"

"This is about Jacob, isn't it?" she sputtered. "Tell me you found who did it."

"Not quite, unfortunately," Calvin said. "Could we come in?"

Marcy sniffled, but held the door open for them. Taylor and Calvin stepped into the modern-style apartment. Art hung on the gray walls, along with Jacob's degree and photos of him and Marcy, looking like a happy young couple. There wasn't a speck of dust on the furniture and the apartment had hardwood floors with high ceilings, night and day from the house Jacob's parents lived in. Taylor figured he either wanted to erase most of where he came from, or he just let Marcy take control of the decorating.

"You can go ahead and sit down," Marcy said, gesturing to the living room. She hurried to the arm chair, in front of a pile of tissues on the glass coffee table. A man's hoodie—likely Jacob's—was balled on the seat next to her.

Taylor sat on the couch with Calvin beside her. A silence hung between them—Marcy sniffled again, but dabbed her face with a tissue paper. This wasn't going to be easy. Taylor could tell just by looking at Marcy, at this place, that she was madly in love with Jacob—and Taylor suspected she had no clue about his 'extracurriculars.' Unless, of course, Marcy's life was all for show too.

"We'll keep this brief," Taylor began, "as I understand you're still grieving."

"And we're very sorry for your loss," Calvin added.

Marcy nodded and patted her eyes with the tissue. "Thank you."

"Could you tell us a bit about Jacob and your relationship with him?" Taylor asked.

"Well, we met in college," she said. "He was in law school, me in nursing, but we met on campus and just... clicked. I've never met anyone I got along with so quickly and so easily, you know? But Jake was just that type of guy. He was the life of the party, and everyone wanted to be his friend. I felt so lucky to be with him."

"He sounds like a great guy," Calvin said.

Taylor nodded in agreeance, but moved onto the next question. "And did Jacob ever seem off to you, especially in recent years?"

Confusion crossed Marcy's face. "Off? Like, how?"

"Secretive. Maybe he hid his phone, or—"

"No, never. Jake was an open book."

The innocent look in Marcy's brown eyes was convincing, making Taylor feel even worse about having to do this. Clearing her throat, she went on, "And you were aware Jacob often visited his parents, yes?" Taylor asked, and Marcy nodded again. "Did you ever go with him?"

"Only on holidays. Jake liked to visit his parents and get some alone time with them... I didn't want to intrude."

Taylor exchanged an uneasy look with Calvin, who appeared just as uncomfortable. They both knew where this had to go. And Taylor figured it was better to rip the Band-Aid off than take up more of this woman's time.

"Did Jacob ever mention a bar he visited near his parents' area?" Taylor asked. "It was called Jackhammer."

"No...," Marcy's thin, penciled eyebrows pinched.

"Jacob would visit Jackhammer quite often when he went to see his parents," Calvin said. "Actually, he was physically assaulted by a man there sometime last month."

"What?" Marcy exclaimed. "He never told me this! Why would he get in a bar fight? Jake isn't that type at all!"

Taylor's chest tightened. It was time to come clean—to tell Marcy the truth about Jacob. It wasn't easy doing this, and Taylor would rather Marcy never know at all. The last thing she wanted was to disrespect the deceased, but she had to tell her. Because if Marcy knew anything about Jacob's double life—maybe she could help point them in the direction of the killer. Every lead mattered.

"Actually," Taylor said, "we were informed it was a hate crime committed by a homophobic individual who frequents the area, targeting Jackhammer's clientele."

Marcy blinked again, as though utterly clueless. "So, what, Jake was standing up for someone and that guy beat him up?"

"Not exactly," Taylor mumbled. "Jackhammer is a gay bar, and we've ruled out the man who assaulted Jacob as a suspect in his murder. We've also learned that Jacob was a regular at the bar; he had a separate credit card he used to make purchases there."

"So, what," Marcy said, "Jake was there with a friend or something? What are you telling me?"

"I'm afraid not...," Taylor shifted her weight against the couch. "Jacob seemed to go alone when he went to see his parents. It seems he kept it a secret."

More silence. Marcy just blinked, waiting for clarity.

Taylor continued, "We suspect Jacob had a double life, Ms. Garcia. One he kept from his family, and even you."

Finally, it seemed to click, and Marcy stammered, "You're lying. Jake wouldn't go to a gay bar alone. He wouldn't need to. And he definitely didn't have a double life."

"I'm sorry, Ms. Garcia," Calvin said. "We have the card, and footage of Jacob at the bar."

"Bullshit!" Marcy exclaimed.

Taylor wondered if she was lying, if she knew more than she was letting on. But Marcy's brown eyes darted back and forth over the coffee table, and the realization seemed to settle over her like a cloud of dust—things adding up in her head, things she had probably passed off or made excuses for.

Taylor could see it on her face: she really had no idea.

"It can't be true," Marcy muttered, more tears falling down her flushed cheeks. "No… he wouldn't."

"I'm sorry," Taylor said. "If you know anything about this, anything that could help us find out who would want to hurt Jacob, that would be extremely valuable."

"I don't know anything," Marcy said. "How could I? This is the first time I'm even hearing any of this. What would I know? You're coming in here, telling me I knew nothing about my fiancé…" She trailed off, hiding her eyes in her hands.

Taylor looked at Calvin's guilt-ridden face—it probably mirrored her own. One thing was certain: Jacob's fiancé was nothing but a dead end, and they'd made her grieving even worse by telling her this. What weighed on Taylor more was that she had revealed something about Jacob that he had never intended for Marcy to know, and that made her feel dirty. And it didn't even bring her a single step closer to his killer.

"I'm sorry, again." Taylor stood and bowed slightly. "We'll be going. If you come up with anything that might be useful, please reach out."

Marcy only cried more. Leaving her card on the coffee table, Taylor showed herself out, Calvin following.

Back in the hallway, they went for the elevator. Frustration grew inside Taylor as she pushed the button.

"Damn it," she cursed. "All this way, and not a single lead."

The elevator dinged, and the two agents stepped in. As it continued to the bottom floor, Taylor ran over the case in her mind. From Tim Dallas to Marcy Garcia, they had gotten nowhere near closer to Jacob's killer. It felt like walking into a brick wall, over and over again.

But now that Taylor thought about it, coming here and telling Marcy the truth about Jacob was set up to be a failure form the start. When she was digging into Frank Turner last night, there was no evidence to suggest he was gay, which suggested Jacob's sexuality might not have been linked to his death. Also, Jacob left his credit card at his parents' house the night he was killed, which likely meant he wasn't anywhere near Jackhammer.

A grunt of frustration escaped Taylor's lips as she and Calvin exited the building, onto the early morning street, surrounded by D.C.'s historic architecture. Pedestrians passed, going about their normal lives. Sometimes, Taylor envied them. Being an agent was her calling. But it had its tolls.

“Hey, it was worth a shot.” Calvin stuffed his hands in the pockets of his pants. He’d opted for just a white dress shirt and slacks, as it was far too hot and sunny out to endure much else—something Taylor had admittedly planned poorly for, as her blouse was pitch black. Then again, she’d always thought black looked best on her, no matter how blazing the summer sun got.

“Was it, Scott?” Taylor said. “I can’t help but feel like we just wasted time and made someone’s life much more difficult.”

Calvin ran his hand along the back of his neck. “Well…”

As they approached Calvin’s car, parked on the side of the road, a sign up ahead caught Taylor’s eye. It read: CONSIGN/CONSERVE.

She paused.

Just yesterday, Miriam Belasco had read Taylor the cards Four of Pentacles, which means conservation, and Six of Cups, which means moving forward and leaving home. Every day, as Jacob left his home to go about his business, he would walk past this sign with ‘conserve’ in the title.

Odd, Taylor thought. Extremely odd. It was a strange coincidence—but still a coincidence. It had to be.

She continued walking to the car, trying to push it behind her, but the feeling that there could be something there pulled back on her like an anchor.

She could get into Calvin’s car, drive back to Quantico with no more leads, nothing to go on.

Or she could look into the store. Taylor couldn’t believe she was entertaining the idea—but maybe, even on an off chance, it could be worth looking into. There was only one way to find out.

“Scott, I need to check something,” Taylor said. “That store right there, Consign/Conserve. Let’s go in.”

“What for?” Calvin cocked an eyebrow.

Taylor averted her eyes. She couldn’t admit to him her true reasons, as they would sound as crazy to him as they did to her. Tarot cards? Fortune readings? None of these belonged on an FBI case, especially not one so serious.

But as much as it clawed against her beliefs, Taylor needed to know. Just to be sure. *Crazier things could happen.*

“Just follow me,” she muttered and took off down the street.

CHAPTER EIGHT

The door dinged as Taylor entered Consign/Conserve with Calvin behind her. Racks of vintage clothing lined the aisle that led to the cashier's desk, and rows upon rows of old junk—like household appliances and rejected lawn ornaments—stacked the walls. Taylor had always liked the smell of thrift stores—it was comforting, like that old basement smell, but something about this one felt… off. The glassy eyes of a vintage doll shone at her, seeming to follow her as she walked through the store.

An older man, probably in his fifties, stood behind the cash register. A pencil mustache sat on top of his lip, and he was rearranging a stack of withered magazines. His head lifted when Taylor and Calvin approached, badges out, and his face went pale.

"Oh, no—did something happen?" he asked.

"Good morning, sir," Taylor cut in. "Do you mind if we ask you a few questions?"

"I mean, of course," the man said. "I've never had federal agents in my shop before. What's this all about?"

Taylor took out her phone with a picture of Jacob, zoomed in on the torso to show only the dress—not the crime attached to it.

"Does this dress look familiar to you?" she asked, and in her periphery, Calvin glanced at her, probably wondering if she'd lost her mind. Why would this random shop owner, with seemingly no connection to anyone, know anything? It seemed crazy, and Taylor was starting to think the same thing. She made a mental note to not tell Ben that tarot nonsense had gotten into her head.

The worker adjusted his glasses on his nose and squinted at the photo. "I'm afraid not. We sell a lot of dresses here, but that doesn't look familiar to me."

Taylor pulled up the image of Victim One, Frank Turner, and zoomed in on his dress. *Just in case.*

The worker had the same response—a clueless shrug. "Sorry, folks. They could've been in here at some point, but I wouldn't be able to tell ya. We don't have a tracking system for used clothes. I will say, that red one, especially, looks a bit too fancy for us."

Damn it.

"Thanks," Taylor muttered. "We'll just have a look around, see if anything seems familiar."

"Please, take your time!"

Taylor went straight for the back of the shop. Racks of costume dresses and party dresses alike walled her into the aisle. Calvin came up behind her.

"What are you thinking, Agent Sage?" he asked with genuine curiosity—and a bit of fascination—in his voice. "Come on, tell me why you really wanted to come in here."

Taylor ran her hand over the fabric of a sequin dress. She wasn't about to tell Calvin the truth—she'd lose some of his respect as a fellow agent, she was certain of that. But even if this shop didn't give her any answers, this new line of thinking might be a step in the right direction.

After all, the dress Jacob Gregory was wearing was unique: red fabric mixed with lace, and it was clean, remarkably clean. Taylor was no expert on fashion, but she would have guessed it was a high school prom dress, likely new.

"Like I said before," Taylor mumbled, "Jacob's 'other life' doesn't seem connected to Frank Turner, so there's a chance it isn't connected to his death, either. The hate crime theory is quickly dissolving, Scott, and we have nothing… nothing but the dress."

Calvin nodded, and understanding crossed his gentle features. "I think I know where you're going with this. What I don't understand is why you wanted to come into this store specifically, when it's pretty unlikely the killer would've been all the way out here."

"We don't know that. We don't know anything."

"Jacob died in Vernon Lake, not D.C.," Calvin said.

Taylor didn't reply. Calvin sighed, seemingly annoyed by her mystique—but Taylor wasn't going to give him more than that. But taking a look at all of these costume dresses, most of which seemed old, Taylor had an idea. The shop owner had said the dress seemed 'too fancy' to be from here.

But other dress stores would certainly sell something of that caliber. Whether the dress was old or new, factory or custom made, from China or the U.S., would make a difference.

"Do me a favor," she said. "Call forensics and see if we can get an ID on the make of the dress. The age, too. It's important."

"You're the boss," Calvin muttered, and he exited the store, leaving Taylor to continue scanning the aisles for anything that might resemble a clue. There were no other customers, just the worker still at the cash register, unbothered by her presence.

As Taylor looked at the thrift store dresses, she wondered how the killer chose which dress he'd use. The crimes were so deliberate, it didn't seem likely they were chosen at random. Hopefully getting an ID on them would help narrow it down. The dresses were significant—of that, Taylor was certain.

A couple of minutes later, Calvin came back. "They say the dress is dated to the 1990s," he said. "It was made in the US, but the tag at the back is faded. He said something about it starting with an F."

Taylor's brows raised. The '90s? It looked brand new.

"Well, let's—" Taylor began, but Calvin swiftly cut her off by putting his phone in her face. It had a search of dress shops in the area—exactly what Taylor was going to suggest next.

"I do have *some* experience, you know," Calvin grinned. It almost made her smile. Almost.

Agent Scott was no Agent Jenkins, and he was easily the youngest partner she'd ever had, but Taylor had once been the youngest one, too, and she'd appreciated the times her superiors had treated her with mutual respect. Calvin was clearly trying to be an active participant in the case, and he had Taylor's respect for that. And though she wasn't the mushy type, she wanted him to know she appreciated the effort.

So she said, "Good work, Scott. Now let's split up."

***

Two hours later, Taylor hopped outside of a cab, feeling infinitely more frustrated than she had earlier. Three stores down, and she hadn't gotten anywhere—not to mention, there was only one more left on her list. She tipped the driver, and he drove off, leaving her in front of her final destination: Annabelle's.

Vintage gowns were displayed behind the glass window. This was a richer end of town, and the opulence of the dresses reflected that. The sign for the shop was in neat cursive.

Still, Taylor was starting to lose hope this would lead anywhere at all. The other three hadn't yielded even a hint—not a single worker recognized the dress on either Jacob or Frank. *This is grunt work,* she thought. And as she stared down the window of Annabelle's, she was pretty damn close to calling it quits. Some junior agents could be exploring these leads while Taylor focused on the bigger picture. At this point in her career, she was over chasing her tail. Plus, it was getting late; she'd had to take a cab around town, since Calvin had reclaimed his car, and some shops were spread all over D.C. Now, the late afternoon sun was dipping toward the horizon, and Ben would be expecting her home soon.

And yet the inkling that something in D.C. was going to lead her somewhere wouldn't let her walk away. Not yet. Maybe the store hadn't given her a direct lead, but it had got her thinking more clearly about the dress. That had to mean something—right?

God, I'm starting to sound like Ben...

Moving on, Taylor pushed through the glass door of Annabelle's. This worker, unlike the previous people she'd interviewed, was young, and had a classic, Audrey Hepburn-like beauty to her. She wore a simple, yet elegant dress that reminded Taylor of something a flapper might have worn in the 1920s.

At this point, showing her badge and getting up the zoomed-in photos had become a monotonous routine to Taylor. But she went through the beats anyway, cutting to the chase and flashing her badge quick. Like most people so far, the worker looked both surprised and concerned.

"Oh, my, what happened?" she asked.

"Good afternoon, ma'am," Taylor said, trying to hide the apathy in her voice. "I won't take up too much of your time. I was hoping you could help me identify a dress."

Taylor took out the phone with the zoomed-in photo, sparing the girl from having to see the violent crime attached. She leaned in, brows pinched as she observed the scene—the one of Jacob in his red dress—and recognition crossed her face.

"Oh, wow," she said. "That is definitely a Francois Monet."

Taylor's heartbeat increased. She couldn't believe it—it didn't feel real. This was actually leading somewhere. The name starting with F would line up with the partial tag found on Jacob's dress.

"You know this dress?" Taylor asked with bated breath.

"Oh, yes," said the girl. "Francois is a local designer. A strange man, but his work is stunning. That lacework is a tell-tale sign of a Monet dress."

Taylor's palms grew sweaty, and she pulled up the photo of Frank, zoomed-in once again.

"This one is a bit harder to tell," the worker said, "but it could also be a Monet."

"Is there anything else you can tell me about this Francois Monet?" Taylor asked.

He could be our guy. It was too coincidental for him to not be.

"Well, I have to say," the worker said, "I'm not surprised to hear he may be caught up in an FBI investigation. He's an older man, quiet, and quite reserved. He is very prideful when it comes to his work, though."

Taylor thought back to Jacob's crime scene—the precision, the effort that went into prettying him up like a doll. 'Prideful' would be a word that fits.

"Do you know where I might find him?" Taylor asked.

"Actually, I might," the worker said. "He has a showroom just a few blocks over. Here, let me write down the address for you."

She breezed over to the cash counter and picked up one of the store's cards. Taylor watched intently as she jotted down the address, then handed it back to her.

"You should be able to get there in five minutes," the girl said.

Taylor gripped the card tight in her hand. "Thank you," she said to the worker, then she rushed out of the store.

Back on the street, Taylor took out her phone and quickly searched the address. Like the worker said, it was barely a five-minute walk away. She called Calvin, and he answered within a single ring.

"Sage, do you have something? 'Cause I've got nothing—"

"I'm texting you an address," Taylor cut him off. "Get here *now.*"

CHAPTER NINE

Taylor's heart pounded like a drum in her ears. She rushed up the street and around the block, to the address the worker had given her for the dressmaker's showroom.

A peeling FOR SALE sign was pasted in the window. Remnants of graffiti were scribbled on the door, and though it had been mostly scratched off, Taylor could make out one distinct word.

PERVERT.

This could be our guy, she thought. *It has to be.*

Just as she was peering through the glass for further clues, the wheels of Calvin's car skidded to a halt outside of the building. Calvin rushed out. He looked rightfully confused as he jogged up to her and stopped to catch his breath.

"Holy shit," Calvin said as he scanned the abandoned shop, taking in the word on the door. "Who lives here?"

"Apparently, some dressmaker named Francois Monet," Taylor explained. "The last shop I went to ID'd Jacob's dress as a Monet. This used to be his showroom. But as you can see…"

"He's clearly gone," Calvin said.

"Exactly. So let's find out where he went."

They went into Calvin's car, where Calvin pulled out his laptop and began searching the FBI database. Taylor shook with anticipation as she tapped her leg, causing the car to vibrate. Finally, Calvin got some answers.

"Francois Monet. Sixty-three. He lives in Petersburg."

"Okay," Taylor said, buckling her seatbelt, "so let's go."

But Calvin didn't whip the car into drive and start hurrying like Taylor wanted. Instead, he sighed, closing his laptop. "Sage, I've been working with you for barely two days, and I can already tell you're a hell of an agent. But you don't have to work around the clock. If we go now and arrive at night—and this *is* our guy—we could just spook him. And that won't do us much good at all."

Taylor bit her tongue, relaxing against the seat. Calvin was talking sense, but her urge to chase this guy down was like a volcano threatening to burst inside her. How could she just *go home* after a revelation like this?

But then she remembered Ben. At home, waiting, expecting her to keep her promise to return. She had barely spent ten minutes in their new house, while Ben had been there all alone, dealing with the movers and unpacking their stuff.

Calvin had a point. Going now might be reckless. Taylor had never been one to shy away from danger if it meant getting to the truth—and saving lives. But for now, she would let it rest, and first thing tomorrow, she was getting on the road. Francois Monet would still be there.

"All right." Taylor heaved out a sigh. "Let's head back."

But she couldn't shake the feeling this decision would come with a price.

***

When Taylor walked through the front door of her house, the warmth shocked her. Just the day before yesterday, this place had felt empty and foreign; but already, the smell of her and Ben's old home was permeating the air. Especially with the aroma of Ben's spaghetti—red wine, onions, and garlic—simmering throughout.

Many boxes laid unpacked on the floor, some with papers or junk spilling out, but the couches were set up in the living room with the nightstands and lamps on. It was dark outside, but Ben had Taylor's favorite warm lights on, making the house feel cozy.

Taylor stepped into the living room and peered toward the dining room and kitchen. Candles were lit on the table. Plates and cutlery were arranged, and a giant bowl of spaghetti and meatballs sat next to a bowl of Caesar salad with tongs poking out.

He did all this?

Ben came out with a pair of oven mitts on, holding a hot pan of garlic bread. He must not have heard her come in, because he looked at her with wide eyes and said: "Oh, honey! You're right on time!"

"Wow, this looks incredible," Taylor said. "But honey, I never said when I'd be home."

"Well, you promised you'd be back today, and I trusted you to follow through." He placed the garlic bread pan on a cloth on the table and came over to kiss the side of her head. "I knew you would."

Taylor felt terrible for almost considering bailing on him. If she had, he would have done all of this for nothing.

Still, Francois Monet lingered in the forefront of Taylor's mind. She wanted to be at his house right now, banging on his door—but she forced herself to stay in the present, for Ben's sake. At least, she tried to.

Ben gestured for Taylor to take a seat, so she did, and he sat down opposite her. He looked at her with a warm smile, and Taylor tried to return it. But hunting down a killer didn't exactly leave her with a big appetite. Even as Ben loaded spaghetti, salad, and bread on her plate, Taylor caught her mind drifting.

Could Francois Monet really be him? It seems almost too easy. I don't know how Scott could just walk away. What if he kills again? Shit—we should have gone.

"Taylor?" Ben's voice interrupted Taylor's thoughts, and she snapped out of it.

"Yes?"

"Were you listening?" His brows drooped. "I asked if you wanted red or white."

"Oh, sorry, Ben. Red is great."

Ben poured them each a glass of merlot, Taylor's favorite. She took a sip, but couldn't focus. She began eating her meal in silence.

"So, tell me what's going on," Ben began, eating a meatball. "You must be working a major case, yeah?"

"You could say that." Taylor poked at her salad, then met her husband's curious gaze. "Maybe it's best if we don't talk about it."

She was already having a hard enough time focusing on Ben. Talking about the case would only make her want to run back to work even more.

"Well, aren't you going to ask how my work went?" Ben asked.

"I thought you didn't start until tomorrow?"

"Is unpacking all of our stuff and moving all of our furniture alone not work?" His jaw appeared stiff. "I had the movers help me get the heavy stuff upstairs, but… there's still so much to do."

Taylor's chest sank. She knew Ben well enough to sense when he was annoyed, but trying to stay civil. She said, "I'm sorry, honey, just leave some for me and I'll help as soon as I can."

"It's fine, don't worry! I've already unpacked most of the clothes. I found that blue dress you used to wear. You should put it on again, it looks so nice on you."

A dress.

What were the chances Jacob would be found in a Monet dress, a dress made by a man who happened to have a showroom in the town he lived in? Taylor also realized—she hadn't checked the date when the showroom had closed down. She had the urge to text Calvin and ask him to do it, but maybe he was spending quality time with his family too.

"Taylor."

She snapped her head to her husband. Irritation flashed across Ben's face.

"You didn't hear a word I said, did you?" he asked.

Taylor's cheeks flushed. "Ah, I'm sorry—I have a lot on my mind."

"But you don't want to talk about it." Ben placed his utensils down. "I know your work always comes first, but this is your first actual day in our new home—could you at least try to be present?"

Taylor couldn't help the annoyance that flushed through her. "I am trying, Ben. I'm sorry. I do appreciate this, but the case I'm working—"

"Then *talk* to me about it."

She paused. "You know I'd rather keep work and our home life separate."

"But work *controls* our home life." He gestured to the room around them, still full of unpacked boxes. "We left behind a perfectly good home in Portland for your work, Taylor, and you're not even here with me."

A flare of anger struck her. She abruptly stood.

Before they'd moved, Taylor had been extremely concerned that Ben would regret leaving Portland. She'd asked him, over and over again, if he would be okay, and he insisted that he'd be "thrilled" to move with her. She'd sensed sometimes this was off, but had chosen to believe her husband was telling her the truth.

But now, with this coming out, she felt like she'd been lied to.

"You told me you were okay with moving. I asked you many times, Ben. Or was that a lie?"

Disarmed, Ben let out a sigh and rubbed his temples before he met her eyes. "No. It wasn't a lie. I was happy to move, I just want you to actually *be* here."

"You know what my job is like."

"You also said things would be different here. Taylor, we're supposed to be planning for our *family.*"

Feeling cornered, the strong urge to end this conversation took over Taylor. She didn't want to talk about it—or about anything with Ben. She needed to be alone.

So before she hurt his feelings more, she said, "I'm sorry. I think I need to cool off and get some sleep. It's been hard. Leave the dishes for me, I'll clean them in the morning." Despite the tension, Taylor walked around the table and kissed the side of his head. "Thank you, again, and I'm sorry."

Ben didn't reply, and Taylor made her way to the stairs, up to their new bedroom for the first time.

The room contained much of the same stuff from their old place, but even the bedsheets felt foreign to her. Taylor rifled through a box until she found her pajamas and changed into them. But she didn't realize how tired she was until she crawled into bed and her head hit the pillow. Slowly, Taylor drifted away, her mind spiraling around what would happen tomorrow when she finally got to confront Monet.

***

Taylor's eyes popped open to the high ceilings of a warehouse.

She stood, disoriented and delirious. She was surrounded by boxes, and the room stunk of the oil used to grease up the machinery built along the walls.

I've been here before.

But then Taylor remembered—it was one of her first tasks as a new agent. She knew better than to come alone, but she had to prove herself to her superiors. She'd worked so hard to get here and wouldn't be underestimated. If she could crack this case on her own, she'd surely gain the respect and acknowledgement she'd worked so hard to achieve.

Still, Taylor's heart battled her ribcage. She took out her gun, positioned it in her sweaty hands, and quickly moved behind the next row of boxes with her weapon cocked. No one was there, but somehow, Taylor knew this was where she needed to be. She knew whoever she was hunting was around here somewhere.

"This is Special Agent Taylor Sage!" she shouted, gun cocked. She quickly moved behind another row of boxes—still no one. "I'm with the FBI! Come out with your hands up!"

Still, nothing but silence.

That was when Taylor noticed a door across the room. Something about it called to her. Ducked low to avoid any potential attackers, she made her way to the door—but when she turned the knob, it wouldn't budge. Taylor checked over her shoulder, into the empty warehouse. No one was there. So she holstered her weapon and began picking the lock with a bobby pin, as she'd been taught to do in emergency situations.

Despite her shaking hands, Taylor managed to get the lock. She felt the satisfying *click* behind the knob and sighed in relief.

She turned the door and opened it, when—

BANG.

Everything went black.

When Taylor opened her eyes again, she was lying on the cold, concrete floor. The sound of the gunshot resonated through her mind, and she clutched at her abdomen. A searing pain like she'd never felt before penetrated her, assaulting every nerve in her body.

Warm blood oozed from the wound. Taylor tried desperately to stop the bleeding with her clothes, hands, anything—but it wouldn't stop gushing.

No, not there, not there!

She was bleeding out, losing so much blood that she'd surely die. But Taylor didn't care about her own life. All she cared about was the tiny life that had been growing inside her. Inside her uterus.

Right where the gun had pierced.

Another bang, and Taylor jolted upright—only to see the room had changed.

The warehouse faded, and her room at her new house with Ben materialized before her eyes.

A ringing was coming from the cell phone on the nightstand beside her bed. Taylor lifted up the shirt of her pajamas and clutched at the scar on her abdomen—no bleeding.

Just a dream. I'm fine. Just a dream.

But it was more of a memory, and it shocked Taylor how real it had felt, like she had truly been there again, reliving that awful experience.

Heart still hammering, Taylor tried to catch her breath. The clock read six a.m.—Ben hadn't come to bed.

The ringing continued, and Taylor snapped out of her trance. She grabbed her phone to see the caller ID: Calvin Scott. Her pulse, yet again, quickened. Calvin wouldn't be calling so early for no reason. Taylor quickly pressed accept and placed the phone to her ear.

“This is Agent Sage,” she said, trying to hide the sleep in her voice.

“Sage,” Calvin’s voice came through the phone. Oddly enough, it was nice to hear after that nightmare she’d just experienced. It grounded her back to reality. “I hope I’m not waking you. We have a situation.”

“What is it, Scott?”

He paused, and each microsecond caused Taylor’s anxiety to increase tenfold, before Calvin’s voice came in with: “The visit to the dressmaker today is gonna have to wait a bit. You were right, Sage.”

She swung her legs around the bed and stood up, anticipating Calvin’s next words with bated breath, until he said:

“They’ve found another body.”

CHAPTER TEN

When Taylor arrived at the scene, dawn painted the sky in plumes of orange and pink—but the good weather did nothing to ease her mind. As she pulled into the lot of the public park, her knuckles turned white on the steering wheel of her car.

Another body. We should've acted sooner.

Damn it!

This was her fault. She couldn't shake the guilt. Even if the dressmaker wasn't their guy—if Taylor had acted faster, figured out who the killer was sooner, another person wouldn't have lost their life.

She veered into a parking spot and quickly shut off the car, then hurried out as fast as she could. The early morning sun rose above the trees and warmed her blouse as she jogged toward the scene, where she made out Calvin's tall form in the distance, standing with other officers behind a caution taped area.

Taylor jogged up to the park bench, but slowed as the crime came into sight. Her stomach lurched.

This made the previous killings look like child's play.

The body of a young man was elaborately staged with his feet on the ground, his back on the bench in a strange, bent backwards position. The killer would have needed to take extra time positioning the feet so that gravity would keep the corpse upright.

And the face—his mouth was taped back in that wide grin that made Taylor's skin crawl, but somehow, this time, he'd tied the tape tighter, made the smile wider.

But what shocked her the most was the blood. The previous two men had been killed quietly, a single stab wound to their chests—but this was violent. Blood stained the white lacy dress, splotches all over the torso to the point that the murder itself must have been completely overkill. Taylor pictured the knife going into the man's chest, over and over again, long after he was dead.

This was far too elaborate, too deliberate. The killer was trying to make a statement—but what? It almost felt like a taunt, as if to say, *"Look, you can't catch me; I'm capable of so much worse."*

Taylor's teeth grit. If this was how fast the killer was moving—she could only imagine what the next crime would look like.

We have to stop him before it's too late again.

Calvin came over to Taylor, and his face mirrored her own guilt. He stuffed his hands in the pockets of his suit pants. Neither of them spoke—their mutual guilt was wordless between them. They each stared at the body, taking in the details.

Eventually, Taylor asked, "When did this happen?"

"It was reported around 5:35 a.m.," Calvin said. "Some kids out drinking found the body like this. I got the call, called you immediately, and here we are."

It was pushing 6:30 a.m. This town was about an hour out from Pelican Beach. Taylor had sped, so she had made it here in forty-five.

"I keep trying to come up with a profile for this guy," Calvin said, "and I've got nothing. What's he trying to say?"

Taylor was trying to figure that out too. Eyes skating over the scene, she let her thoughts wander.

The victim was, of course, another young man. Taylor saw an obsession with youth. With beauty. Femininity. For one, she felt he was trying to flaunt how he could get away with it. Like he could kill three men, one of them brutally, and still not get caught. He was escalating, and he was escalating fast—Taylor couldn't help but think he was dangling it in their faces. But it was more than that. This crime felt too passionate to simply be directed at police. It was so intricate, so *personal,* like the act of an angry broken heart.

Could that be what this is about?

She stepped in for a closer look, focusing on the blood splatter and the curved angle of the victim's spine.

The fact that each crime has taken place in a different small town, but all within the same vicinity, told Taylor two things.

One: he likely lived somewhere around here.

Two: if he was trying to send a message, it wasn't to the people of any specific town.

So who was it for, then? Could it be to warn all young men throughout this half of the state that they aren't safe?

Shutting her eyes, Taylor thought back to the two previous crimes. The elegant dresses, mixed with the messy makeup and sinister smiles…

There was something, for lack of a better term, romantic about these crimes. Taylor turned to Calvin—maybe he'd have his own insight on the situation.

"Could it be about heartbreak?" she asked.

Calvin lifted an eyebrow, hands in the pockets of his pants. "How do you mean?"

"Well, I'm not so sure… but think about it. The first two victims were men dressed as women, with stab wounds to their chests. You know, where their hearts were. This one, however, is violent, passionate… but that doesn't mean the killer doesn't view it as some sort of love."

"What are you getting at, Sage?"

"And the smeared lipstick, too—even in the last two scenes, it felt passionately violent." Taylor paused. She wasn't sure Calvin was following—but decided to roll with her theory, which was quickly building in her head. She continued, "Maybe he was cheated on by a woman, and now he is enacting his revenge on men by killing them and dressing them like the woman who hurt him."

Calvin didn't look convinced. Taylor wasn't, either, but this train of thought was leading somewhere—she could feel it.

"But why not just kill women?" Calvin asked. "Unfortunately, that's usually what we see."

"Maybe he didn't blame—or hate—the woman. Maybe he hated the man. Or maybe, he is gay, and we're looking at a Dahmer situation. I don't have the answers yet, Scott, but I guess where I'm really going with this is that something tells me we're dealing with someone who has a very cynical outlook on love and relationships. Something about these killings feels more romantic, for lack of a better word, than sexual. But it also feels vengeful."

Calvin nodded, understanding crossing his features. "Okay, yeah, I can see that."

Regardless of the killer's psych profile, there was one thing that would determine—without a doubt—who they needed to visit next.

Taylor slid on a black glove and stepped toward the body. She'd been close to many corpses in her life, but that never made approaching one any more pleasant. She held her breath, so as not to inhale any scents.

"Sage, what are you doing?" Calvin asked, but Taylor didn't reply—he'd see soon enough. She carefully approached the victim, chilled by the look in his dead, glazed-over eyes. Seeing a *young* person dead was always even more difficult to handle; something about it felt so unnatural, like the brain couldn't process the sight the same way it might process an elderly person.

Taylor lowered beneath the curve of the victim's spine. Careful not to upset the scene, she checked the tag

Exactly as she'd thought.

Francois Monet.

***

Taylor's hands trembled with anticipation as she and Calvin walked up the cobblestone driveway of Francois Monet's Petersburg house. It was made mostly of vintage stonework, but the various sculptures and elegant plants gave it a showy, arthouse vibe. The early afternoon sun shone high above the chimney, which had plumes of smoke piling into the sky from it.

It had taken them two hours to get there, and to say Taylor was anxious the whole time would be an understatement. At least this time, she was driving, so she had been able to focus on the road as a distraction.

But finally, they were here. And finally, she could confront the person who had been plaguing her mind for the past twenty-four hours—somehow, it felt like she'd waited even longer just to arrive.

Taylor rapped three hard knocks at the door. Moments passed before a man in his sixties answered. He was short and thin, with posture so straight he reminded Taylor of a mannequin. There was not a hair on his face, aside from his trimmed eyebrows, and he looked at them beneath thick-rimmed glasses.

For a moment, Taylor was sure she saw apprehension on his face. But then she said, "Good afternoon, sir. You're Francois Monet, yes?"

"Yes…." he said. "I don't recall scheduling any tours today."

He does tours of his house? Taylor thought. Seems awfully narcissistic…

"Actually, we're with the FBI," Taylor said, showing her badge. Calvin did the same, and Monet's face dropped. Taylor continued, "We're investigating the graffiti done to your showroom in D.C."

Monet's tense body unwound a bit. Then, his brows went up in surprise. "That's a long way to come just for some graffiti."

"Well, we're looking into a series of similar cases," Calvin said. "Mind if we come in?"

Monet's eyes flicked between them—distrusting. "Of course… let me give you a tour."

They stepped inside. Taylor's first thought was that it was clean—too clean. The hardwood floor was immaculately polished, and a chandelier hung from the high ceiling of the foyer. A cloth mannequin sporting a lacy dress was positioned beside several black and white photographs of women in dresses which, Taylor could only assume, were all designed by Monet.

One thing was for sure: the man was proud of his work.

"Not only is this my home," Monet said, "but it is also my home studio. On your right, there, you'll see my main dressing room."

Through a glass door on the right were more mannequins wearing dresses.

"Once I have something fully designed," Monet said, "I take it in there to try out."

When neither Taylor nor Calvin replied, Monet's lips pursed; he seemed irritated they didn't show more interest in his work. Excessive pride was an easy trait of the psychopath.

"Is it just you here?" Taylor asked. "Any kids? Pets?"

She swore she smelled animals. Ben's parents were dog lovers, and the house had that smell—and yet, she saw no evidence of any pets. No dog hairs on the tile or leashes hanging on the coat rack.

"No, just me here," Monet said. "Come on, we can have a chat somewhere more comfortable."

Quietly, Taylor and Calvin followed Monet through a long hallway, that felt more like a corridor. It was fairly open and bright, with many windows, and most doors had glass panels so Taylor was able to see inside. They seemed to be mostly spare rooms, or more space for mannequins.

But one door had no glass at all—it was just solid white. And it was closed.

It could be nothing, but Taylor jumped at her chance to ask: "What's behind this door, Mr. Monet?"

"Hmm?" He looked at her over his shoulder. "Oh, that's nothing. Just old storage…"

Monet averted his eyes. Taylor nodded, trying to look like he'd convinced her—but something felt off. In fact, everything in this house was off.

"Anyway," Monet said, gesturing to a door up the hall, "if you'd just step into my living room, we can discuss the graffiti incident."

Taylor and Calvin followed into a small, cozy living room with red velvet couches—not at all cheap. Monet clearly made a killing off his dresses. In every room were more and more photographs of different women wearing his work. Taylor and Calvin sat on the couch opposite Monet's loveseat, backdropped by a large brick fireplace that was not lit.

"We won't take up too much of your time," Taylor said. "Can you tell us why someone might have painted that word on your shop?"

"It was all a misunderstanding, you see." Monet crossed his legs over his suit pants. "A woman hired me to design a custom prom dress for her teenage daughter, but she didn't seem to understand how custom dressmaking works. When I went to take her daughter's measurements, she went completely off the rails and accused me of being, well…"

"A pervert," Taylor said. "Like the graffiti suggested."

"Yes." Monet's head hung low. "It was awful. And the news spread all throughout the girl's high school, so of course, the other students began to view me as such…"

As Monet spoke, Taylor couldn't stop thinking about the door—and his reaction to it. She'd dealt with enough liars throughout her years, and that reaction—while subtle—was a tell-tale sign.

I need to check it out… just in case.

While Monet was mid-sentence, saying something to Calvin, Taylor cut in with: "Sorry, do you mind if I use your restroom? It's been a long drive."

She glanced at Calvin, who raised an eyebrow—they'd stopped at a coffee shop right before coming, so there was no reason for Taylor to need the bathroom again. She hoped the non-verbal communication was enough to send the message: *Stall him!*

"Of course, dear," Monet said. "It's down the hall on the left."

Taylor nodded and scurried out of the room.

Once in the hall, away from Monet's eyes, she took a deep breath and listened. Calvin must have gotten the hint, because he said, "So you design all these dresses yourself, huh?"

Taylor took her chances and slipped down the hall, right to the closed door. She glanced over her shoulder before she opened it, and immediately, she was met with a dark room—and a multitude of sounds: pattering on metal, and the distinct smell of animals assaulted her nose, reminding her of the last time she stepped foot in an animal shelter. She reached out for a light switch on the wall—and when she flicked it, she wasn't prepared for what she was about to see.

Every inch of the room was lined with cages, each one containing a living creature. Some tiny and furry, others larger, and one was even a mammal with scales—a pangolin. A cacophony of hissing and growling bombarded her. Taylor took a step closer, and a panic stirred in the room. She flinched when an animal near her leg slammed at the bars and bared its sharp teeth.

Taylor was no expert on animals, but she could have sworn it was a mink.

Regardless of what they were, she was damn confident every single one of them was highly illegal to own in America.

The narcissism, the accusations of being a pervert, the dresses on the victims' bodies—and now the proof that he was a criminal. This was all Taylor needed.

Shuffling out of the room, Taylor closed the door behind her. She bolted down the hall, to the living room—and then she appeared in the doorway.

Monet looked at her, pale-faced. Like he'd seen a ghost. A moment of silence followed in which their eyes locked.

Then he ran.

CHAPTER ELEVEN

Son of a bitch! Taylor darted after Monet as Calvin nearly tripped over the coffee table trying to grab him—but Monet slipped out the other door in the room. Taylor hopped the table and barreled after him, her heart pounding. *This is it. We've got him.*

Like hell would she let him get away and hurt another person.

The hallway led to the kitchen. Monet threw down a potted plant in an attempt to stop the agents, but all it did was shatter on the floor, spilling dirt and ceramic everywhere. Taylor jumped over the mess with ease, Calvin close behind.

Monet booked it into the backyard. Taylor followed. He snaked through the garden, past the birdbath—but when he scrambled toward the fence, Taylor was right on him.

She tackled him from behind, pinning his frail frame to the grass. Within seconds, she'd strapped the cuffs around his wrists.

"All right, all right!" he exclaimed. "I did it, okay? I did it!"

Taylor tightened the cuffs, causing Monet to writhe in pain. Good. Call it sadistic, but after spending the last few days looking into the lives of dead men, she wanted the one responsible to hurt.

She began reading his rights, trying to keep her own anger at bay. "Francois Monet, you have the right to remain silent. Anything you say can and will be used against you in a court of law."

Calvin caught his breath beside them as Taylor pulled an ashamed-looking Monet to his feet.

"I'm sorry!" Monet exclaimed. "I—I swear, I didn't want anyone to get hurt, but—"

"You didn't want anyone to get hurt?" Taylor's teeth grit. Rage began to cloud her eyes. "Do you have any idea what you've done? Jacob Gregory had a family, a fiancé—"

"What?" Tears streamed down Monet's blubbery-red face. "Who on Earth is Jacob Gregory?"

Taylor's chest sank. She exchanged an uneasy look with Calvin.

"The man you killed," Taylor said. But uncertainty laced her voice.

Monet was confessing to the killings—wasn't he?

But Monet looked completely aghast. *"Kill anyone?* I never killed anyone!"

With pinched brows, Calvin crossed his arms over his chest. "What exactly do you think we're here for?"

"The woman here," he said, gesturing his shoulder at Taylor, "she found the animals…"

"What were the animals for?" Taylor's grip tightened on Monet's arm, as if to remind him of his position. Clearly, he was doing something nefarious with them, and Taylor didn't think it was a far stretch from animal killer to human killer.

"I swear, they were just for material," Monet sputtered. "Many of my clients want luxury fur without the price tag that comes with extensive regulations. I knew it was wrong, but I could make so much more off each dress with these unique furs. Chinchillas, minks—I even have clients who want the scales from pangolins… it's wrong, so wrong, but this house—it isn't cheap."

Taylor stood in front of a sulking Monet, forcing eye contact. "Your dresses have been found on the bodies of at least three murdered young men."

"And you think *I* did it? I would never desecrate my own art… that is completely foul!"

Blabbering like an idiot, Taylor thought. *I don't buy this. I can't.*

Everything pointed straight to Monet being the killer—but had Taylor been wrong, yet again? Her skin grew clammy at the idea she'd wasted more time, that the real killer was still out there, hunting his next victim.

Damn it. It has to be him.

"Where were you on Wednesday night?" Taylor questioned.

"I was at home!"

"Can anyone confirm that?"

"W-well, no, but…"

"And what about last night?" Calvin cut in.

Monet's blue eyes were wide, desperate beneath his glasses. "Ah, my show! A hundred people were there—they can confirm it! I swear, I didn't kill anyone!"

Taylor hated the desperation in his voice—and hated even more that she was starting to entertain the idea that maybe it really wasn't him. He seemed like a fool, and also, he was so weak and easy to pin down—could a frail sixty-three-year-old man really be capable of hauling young men's bodies around like the killer had been?

Either way, they were booking him for the illegal fur farm. Whether or not he was their killer was yet to be decided—but Taylor prayed he was.

If she'd just wasted more time chasing down another false lead, she didn't know how she'd ever sleep again.

***

Taylor drummed her fingers against the desk at the Quantico headquarters, laptop open in front of her. She was alone in the room—Calvin was out getting updates on Monet, and Taylor was trying to figure out their next best move. Monet didn't have an alibi for Jacob Gregory's murder, but he insisted on having one for last night. It just needed to be confirmed.

Taylor truly thought the dresses would lead them somewhere, and even if Monet was a dead end—maybe they still could. After all, the dresses were still his work, so the killer must have been an ardent fan.

On her laptop, Taylor scrolled through the internet, looking for places that sold Monet dresses. He was surprisingly popular, with a big name around custom high school prom dresses—at least until the 'incident' involving the teenage girl. Despite that, he'd made a name for himself in a niche crowd of designers, and obviously those who still enjoyed fur, despite most of North America collectively deciding fur in general was in bad taste.

Monet dresses could be found in boutique shops around the state, but his custom business had boomed in D.C. Pinpointing a location of a fan based on that would prove difficult, as really, they could be anywhere. He had managed to weasel his way into quite a few industries.

Before she could finish her thought, Calvin walked briskly into the room.

"Two things," he said. "The good news: The dresses on both Frank Turner and Jacob Gregory are confirmed to be Monet's work. The bad news: Monet's alibi for last night checks out. He had a showing last night in his town, dozens of witnesses confirmed it. He also stayed out late drinking wine with a few friends afterward and fell asleep at his local showroom there. Several witnesses confirmed that too."

Taylor's jaw tensed. "Then he isn't our guy."

"Probably not."

Damn it. Taylor rested her forehead on her palms and closed her eyes, taking comfort in the darkness. Their work wasn't over. Not even close.

As Taylor opened her eyes again, Calvin sighed and sat down across from her. When he added nothing, Taylor went back to her laptop, searching more on Monet's work. If he didn't do it himself, he was still the biggest clue they had yet. One of these results had to yield something.

Calvin broke the silence. "Hey, look, Sage…" He ran his hand along the back of his neck and nervously met her eyes. "I don't mean to step out of line, but are you okay?"

Taylor blinked. "I'm fine, Scott. Just want to keep digging up dirt on Monet and see where it leads us so this doesn't feel like a total waste of time. Why?"

"No, really. You seem tired. Did you even eat today?"

Did she eat? Yes, she had a muffin when they arrived at the station. But Taylor *was* tired—after all, she barely slept, and after the fight with Ben…

It was then she realized she hadn't thought about Ben once that day. Not even for a fleeting second.

Guilt sank her heart, but this wasn't out of character for her and she knew it. Taylor had always had a tendency to become obsessed with her cases—it was part of what made her a good agent, but had never been very good for her social life or relationships. Friendship-wise, she'd always been a lone wolf, though she'd had a few romantic partners come in and out of her life. Only the ex she'd dated before Ben had been truly important to her, and she rarely thought about him at all.

But Ben was the love of her life. If she didn't believe that, she wouldn't have married him. He was a good, moral man. She knew he had needs, and if she didn't try to make a compromise, he'd be even more hurt than he already was.

I should at least send him a text and apologize for leaving so suddenly this morning. Especially after our fight.

Calvin interrupted her thoughts, saying, "I know we just started working together, but I can already tell you're a good agent, Sage. You aren't just in this for a paycheck. You really want to save lives."

Taylor couldn't resist the flush to her cheeks. She was not good at taking compliments, and didn't get why Calvin was suddenly giving her one. "Of course I do, Scott. Don't you?"

"Yeah, I do, but even I find time to eat during the day."

Taylor didn't reply, hoping he'd back off. But he didn't.

"How'd you end up in this field, anyway?" he asked.

This was getting too personal, too fast. Taylor had many reasons for why she'd ended up an agent. For one, she'd been fascinated by serial killers—and the way their minds work—since she was a child. Her father, being a skilled clinical psychologist, had raised her to understand the human mind. What makes people empathetic—and what makes them "evil."

Evil didn't mean someone with poor life circumstances who ended up in a life of crime. No, evil was senseless—it was the desire to kill, to defile, to overpower other people, sometimes to feel powerful, sometimes for no reason at all. That was how Taylor defined evil, and that was what she sensed they were dealing with on this particular case.

However, there was another fact that had led Taylor on her concrete path to law enforcement.

And that was her sister, Angie.

Taylor's heart sank, deep within her chest. Angie's face flashed her mind. She hadn't thought about her in so long, mostly because it hurt too much. Angie had looked much like Taylor—black hair, pale skin, and the trademarked steely gray eyes they inherited from their father. But the difference between them was, Angie had more light in her than darkness. She moved through life with a smile, while Taylor had always been quiet, her nose buried in a book throughout school.

But as the years went on, Taylor's memories of who her sister was were admittedly fading.

Because when Taylor was fourteen, and Angie was sixteen, Angie went missing. Vanished without a trace.

The running theory was that she was abducted on her way home from school, and so like any decent town would for any child, the community got together and started looking. Three days of vigorous searching by both friends and strangers led nowhere. But on the fourth day, K-9 units found a sweater deep in the woods with blood on it.

They confirmed it to be Angie's.

From that point on, Angie was presumed dead. But a body was never found. All these years later, not a trace of her was ever recovered beyond that sweater.

Part of Taylor still hoped, deep within her, that Angie could still be alive out there. More naïvely, she'd hoped over the years that one of her cases may cause her to unwittingly stumble across a clue in Angie's case. But nothing ever came out of it, and now, most days, Taylor tried not to think about her sister at all.

But her case had been the one thing that truly made Taylor want to become an agent—not just a cop, but an actual FBI agent who would hunt down the type of evil that stole her sister and make sure it never happened to another family. No one had the right to take another's life. Taylor believed that to her core.

Pulling herself from the memory, she was brought back to the briefing room with Calvin staring at her, waiting for an answer. Taylor wasn't about to tell him any of that. She hadn't opened up to many people in general, let alone someone she'd known for barely two days. Back in Portland, Agent Jenkins had been the type to never ask questions anyway, so he never tried much to dig beneath Taylor's shell. She sensed Calvin would prove different.

"It just isn't right," was all she said.

"I agree." He went somber for a moment, looking like he was reliving a memory, too. "Look, Sage…," he trailed off.

Taylor lifted an eyebrow. "What?"

She could tell Calvin had something more to add—it was written all over his face. She impatiently waited, until she grew too restless—she had work to do, and he was distracting her.

"If you're not going to say anything, I'd like to keep working," Taylor said.

Calvin looked dejected, but nodded. "Uh, yeah. Of course." He leaned back in his chair, crossing his hands behind his head, but it seemed like he was trying to force himself to act natural. "Any ideas where to go from here? Because I'm stumped. I really thought those dresses would lead us somewhere."

"Maybe they still could. I've been thinking we should go back to the psychological angle. Look into the types of fans Monet has, who the top buyers of his dresses are."

"Some of the witnesses seemed like aristocrat types," Calvin shrugged. "Others, simply artsy fartsy types."

Taylor nodded. "Plus, the rich moms who want their daughters to have the best dress at the prom."

"Or the dads."

A moment of silence spread between them. Taylor was sure the dresses were a hard clue, but she still couldn't place her finger on what they meant. As much as it irked her, they were back to the drawing board—and so she got up and approached the cork board Winchester had showed them before. She flipped it over, revealing the two photos of Frank Turner and Jacob Gregory, before she tacked the photo of their latest victim—Brent St. Clair—to the board.

Calvin stood beside Taylor, and they both observed the photos.

The first victim, Frank, was slightly slumped over on the park bench.

The second victim, Jacob, as stiff as a mannequin.

And the third, Brent, with his bent spine.

"It isn't just the manner of the killings escalating," Taylor said, "it's the positioning, too. It feels like a message. I just don't know what."

"Neither do I," Calvin said.

Taylor walked back over to the desk and picked up the file on Brent St. Clair.

It wasn't just the brutal manner of his death, or the position of his body that was different—it was who he was, too. He was still a young man, only twenty-six years old, but unlike Frank and Jacob, Brent had been a father, and he was leaving behind a wife of three years. Their little girl was only four. Taylor's stomach churned; this next one wasn't going to be easy.

"His MO has shifted each time," Taylor said. "First, a drifter, then a man with a fiancé, and now a father with a wife and child. It might be nothing, but we better be sure." She slung her bag over her shoulder and stood. "Let's go talk to the widow and see if anything connects him to the other two men."

CHAPTER TWELVE

A new development of suburban homes passed beyond the window of the car as Taylor drove, each a near replica of the other. They were on the street Brent St. Clair had lived on, and it became even more evident to Taylor how different this man was as opposed to the previous two victims. Beneath the late-afternoon sun, the grass on each lawn was fresh and green, and sidewalk chalk from children was scribbled all over the pavement. Brent was living the white-picket fence dream. Nothing like Frank, the drifter, and Jacob, the secretive fiancé.

They arrived outside of Brent's house, and Taylor parked on the road. The faint yellow dust of a former hopscotch board was drawn on the driveway.

Taylor had endured many heartbreaking scenes throughout her career; she'd interviewed the families of many people who had lost fathers, mothers, sisters, brothers—and she'd even interviewed the families of killers themselves, people who had no idea the monster they were living with.

That was, unfortunately, all too common.

But talking to families who'd lost a loved one to a violent crime was always worse, especially when a young child was left behind. Taylor didn't want to knock on their door—but knew she had to.

Taylor and Calvin exited the car and walked briskly up to the door. This time, they had decided to call ahead, to give Brent's widow a head's up they were coming. So when Taylor knocked on the door, and the widow answered, she was expecting them.

She was a young blonde woman who instantly gave off a maternal aura. Her blue eyes were devastated, but she held herself together as she took in the two agents on her porch. This was Annie St. Clair, Brent's wife.

"Thank you for coming," she said. "Please, come in."

Nodding, Taylor stepped inside, followed by Calvin, enveloped by the warmth of the home. The house smelled of candles and bread, and it was messy in a way that showed it was properly lived in: books stacked haphazardly on a console table, too many jackets piling on the coat rack.

The living room was divided into two parts: one half dedicated to the television and couches, the other an open area with building block mats on the floor and children's toys scattered about. In the middle of the chaos was a little girl with wispy blonde hair, who didn't even look over as she stacked blocks.

Taylor's heart sank into her stomach, but she did everything to not show how much this scene affected her. Leaving behind something like this was one of her nightmares. She worked a dangerous job—the potential for sudden death came with the territory. And in truth, it was one of the main reasons why she hesitated on having her own kids. She didn't like to admit it, but it did play a factor, even though she'd decided long ago that she did want children someday. But when would 'someday' come?

In her mind, Taylor saw quick flashes. Her new home in Pelican Beach. A phantom child without a face.

Ben.

In her vision, Taylor wasn't there. Ben sat and played with the child on mats like the one Annie's child was playing on now.

But then there was a knock at the door, and Ben answered to see Calvin Scott standing with Steven Winchester, looking downcast as it rained outside. And then Winchester uttered the words, *"We're sorry, Mr. Chambers… Taylor was killed in the line of duty."*

She snapped out of it, into the present. Why the hell was she picturing such depressing situations? It would do her no good—she had a job to get done.

Forcing herself into reality, Taylor kept her gaze firm, her posture strong as she sat next to Calvin on the St. Clairs' couch. She was starting to grow weary of sitting and talking to people—she wanted action. Real progress. And she prayed Annie could help her find it.

"Can you tell us about your husband?" Taylor asked.

Annie tugged at the sleeves of her shirt with her palms, hiding her hands with them. "I wouldn't even know where to begin. He was an amazing father first—Katie loved him." She sniffled, averted her eyes. "An amazing husband, next. He never strayed from me. Not once."

"And do you know where he might have been last night?"

"He was working late—he's a paramedic, so it isn't unusual for him to work overtime." She hung her head low in shame. "When he didn't come home, I wasn't worried."

A heavy silence flowed into the room. The daughter, Katie, kept playing with her toys.

It was probably a shot in the dark, but since Monet's work had been linked to each crime, Taylor decided to give it a try. She adjusted her legs on the couch and asked, "Mrs. St. Clair, are you familiar with a dressmaker by the name of Francois Monet?"

Annie frowned in confusion. "No, why?"

"He's a person of interest in the case. His alibi for the night your husband passed away checks out, but his work has been linked to the crimes, and we're trying to figure out why." A pause—Taylor exchanged a glance with Calvin, who looked curious where she was going with this. Taylor refocused on Annie. "I was curious if you or your husband knew anyone who might have an interest in something like that. Designer dresses, that is."

Annie just shook her head, clueless. "No… not that I can think of. We wanted to get Katie into modeling someday, and Brent mentioned he had an acquaintance who's an expert on that stuff… but that's the closest I can think of. He never mentioned anything specifically about dresses or anyone named Monet."

"Do you know that acquaintance's name?" Taylor asked.

"No, sorry… Brent might have the information somewhere, but he wasn't really a techy guy, and he was very unorganized, so I don't know if he even would have his number saved."

Taylor nodded. Of course this would go nowhere. It was unlikely the killer personally knew any of these victims, as they were all from different towns, and all different in their natures.

Right now, the only thing they had in common was that they were men.

"We don't want to take up too much of your time," Calvin said. "We just wanted to get a feel for your husband's life. Is there anything else you think might be helpful?"

"Did he ever act strange, or feel like he was being watched?" Taylor cut in.

"No. He left for work with a smile and always came back the same way. Trust me, everything was normal. We were happy." Tears escaped her eyes, and she patted them away with her sleeves. "I heard two other men were killed in a similar way."

A pause, and Calvin said, "That's correct."

Silence. Taylor hated that she didn't have more answers for this woman. She hated that she hadn't figured this out yet—if she had, Brent St. Clair wouldn't be dead, and that little girl would still have a father.

A thought crossed Taylor's mind—that even though they still had no real direction, as Francois Monet wasn't their killer, they were still closer than they were before. All because they had chosen to go into that thrift shop. All because that fortune teller had drawn Taylor the Four of Pentacles and Six of Cups.

I can't believe I'm thinking about her again. But as much as Taylor wanted to believe it meant nothing, she couldn't deny the coincidence.

And the fact that the last time she had seen a tarot reader, before Miriam Belasco, back when she was in her twenties, had ended in disaster.

Feeling uneasy in her own skin, Taylor stood. "Thank you for time. And I'm very sorry for your loss."

"Please give us a call if you think of anything that might help us track Brent's movements last night," Calvin said, standing too. "We'll be looking into it as well."

"Of course," Annie said. "I'm sorry I couldn't help more."

They made their way to the front door, past the oblivious little girl. Calvin was saying something else to Annie, but his words tuned out as Taylor's vision zeroed in on the little girl.

She sat upright, playing with a doll in a ruby dress. She combed her tiny fingers through the doll's hair and smoothed it down, before she adjusted the dress around the doll's shoulders.

A light touch to Taylor's back jolted her from the trance. Calvin wore concern in his eyes.

Slightly embarrassed, Taylor nodded at Annie and gave her a stiff smile, before she followed Calvin outside of the house, into the warm day. It was getting late now—almost five p.m., and the sun would soon set.

As they approached her car, parked on the side of the road, Taylor couldn't shake the image of that little girl with her doll. Something about it stood out to her—she just couldn't place what.

Taylor moved to the driver's side of the car while Calvin approached the passenger's side. But before getting in, Calvin said to her over the roof, "Hey, we should probably call it a day, huh? It's getting late."

Taylor paused. She wasn't ready to stop working. How could she rest after all of that?

Calvin clearly sensed her disdain, because he said, "We don't have any concrete leads, Sage. We're tired, and I don't know about you, but

I need to eat. I don't like it either, but you should go home to your husband."

"Do you have someone waiting at home for you, Scott?" she asked, deflecting.

He laughed once, showing his dimples. Sometimes, in certain lights, he seemed so boyishly young, even though he was nearly thirty. "Only a cat named Whiskers, but he needs company too."

Taylor sighed and slid into the car. Calvin got in after her.

"All right," she breathed out. "I'll drop you off at the station."

But Taylor had no intention of going home—not yet.

There was one more place she had to check, if anything, to follow up on this annoying gut feeling.

Miriam Belasco's.

***

It was almost six p.m. when Taylor made it into Pelican Beach, and long shadows stretched over the downtown streets. She'd parked in a lot up the street, and now hurried down the strip to where Belasco's shop was so she wouldn't miss her.

She made it to the door just as Belasco was leaving and locking up the shop. Like last time, Belasco was wearing an extravagant outfit of flowing silks, purple and gold. A look of surprise crossed her features when she saw Taylor approach.

"Mrs. Sage!" Belasco exclaimed. "I didn't expect to see you again, especially so soon."

Taylor felt like an idiot for coming here, but put her own pride aside. Whether she liked it or not, her last reading had opened up another avenue in the investigation. Maybe it meant nothing, but with no more leads to chase, Taylor had nothing to lose.

"Right," she muttered, "I, um. I was actually hoping for a reading."

Belasco lifted her nose and peered at her through curious eyes. "Hmm, I was just closing up, but I could certainly make time for you. Something tells me you've been through a lot since we last spoke."

"Yeah… something like that."

They went inside, where the smell of burnt-out incense still lingered in the air. The place still gave Taylor the creeps, but she followed Belasco behind the curtain, to the table where she and Ben had sat last time.

As before, Taylor sat on one side, Belasco on the other. They spoke no words as Belasco shuffled the cards, and the silence unnerved Taylor more—almost like Belasco knew why she was there without it even being said.

Belasco placed the cards into three decks. Finally, she met Taylor's eyes and said, "Are you ready, Mrs. Sage?"

A lump formed in Taylor's throat, but she nodded.

Belasco flipped the first card. "First, we have Ten of Pentacles, upright. This means legacy, inheritance, and culmination."

Inheritance. That was an interesting word, and it stood out to Taylor. Legacy and inheritance could speak to her of family. Could this killer have a complicated relationship with his parents?

"Next," Belasco said, "we have the King of Wands, upside down. This means impulse, overbearing, and unachievable expectations."

It was like Taylor's thoughts were being read, which frankly, creeped her out. But it intrigued her just the same. Inheritance and unachievable expectations... she didn't have anything to go off right now, but jotted those words down in her mental notebook to revisit when building pathology of the killer.

Belasco paused, then said, "Perhaps this resonates with you. I know you are an FBI agent, after all... I'm sure you've had to face many difficult challenges, not all of which have been successful."

Taylor didn't reply to that, but it got under her skin, mostly because it was true. Of course not every case could be a win. She'd been on this new case for barely two days and a child had already lost her father.

Belasco's hand, with its long, painted fingernails, reached for the third card. Taylor's mouth went dry as she dreaded what it might say. But she had an irking feeling that she already knew.

Belasco flipped the card. Taylor's stomach bottomed out.

Death.

Another death was coming.

CHAPTER THIRTEEN

He liked it when the fabric smoothed between his fingers, lacy threads upon silky gowns. As his hand ran across each garment hanging in the old wardrobe, a warm happiness grew in his stomach.

Who would be the lucky choice tonight?

He stopped at an emerald green gown. *You're perfect.* A smile curled at his lips. He removed the dress, then one by one, packed the supplies into his kit: first the lipstick, then the tape. He'd opted for a shade of ruby red today; it would suit the creamy tone of his guest's skin.

Once fully packed, he went into the next room, where his turntable waited for him to turn on the record. He activated it, and the sound of some good 1940s showtunes flowed through the air, filling the small, dark room. His mother always liked to play them when she put on her makeup, and he'd adopted it as part of his own tradition. She would be proud.

His guest whimpered under his gag beneath the music, but he didn't care; he merely turned with a smile, holding his makeup kit. After hanging the dress on a hook, he stepped closer to his guest.

His guest was bound and gagged, sitting on a chair, and struggled to stand.

Good. I like it when you squirm.

But his guest turned to stone as he approached him, towering over him, feeling so powerful, like a god. He gripped his guest's face firm in his hand to make him stay still before he smeared red lipstick all over his lips. The red spread all over his guest's face, lining up his cleanly-shaved jaw. He'd done that himself, to make him as perfect as he could be. Perfect, like mother wanted *him* to be.

"Good, good," he murmured. Then, he unbound his guest's chest from the chair. His guest looked at him with terror-stricken eyes, as though usure what to do, before he abruptly stood, still gagged with his hand, and went to go run.

He decided not to rush. To give his guest a fleeting moment of joy before he'd take it all away.

Smiling and shaking his head, he allowed his guest to just reach the door, before he stormed over to him.

"Ah, ah, ah!"

The guest froze as the long knife appeared in front of him.

He held it firmly. It gleamed in the single bulb that dangled from the ceiling.

"I'm sorry, you can't leave yet," he said. "But while you're up, why don't you dance for me? Let's see what you can do before we dress you up, hmm?"

The guest remained frozen. Eyes pleading for freedom; a freedom he would never have. But he didn't know that yet.

They would always do anything for hope.

But the guest didn't move. Not even an attempt to get up and dance. Anger clawed through him. This was unacceptable. Was this man going to let them down again, like the last? He couldn't afford another loss.

He grabbed his guest's shoulders and spun him around, hurling him toward the center of the room, next to his chair. "Go on, dance!" he spat.

The guest, whimpering, shuffled his feet.

Relief moved through him. He could relax, only for a moment. He hated when they didn't listen. But so far, his guest was playing along. Was he good enough? He was starting to think the answer would be 'no.'

"No, not like that," he said. "Like *this.*"

He moved his feet as well, like he'd been taught. His guest attempted to match with an awkward flow. Pathetic—this man couldn't dance at all.

A jolt of anger struck him.

"No, you're doing it wrong!" He smacked his guest hard across the face, leaving a giant red mark, and he again whimpered like a cowering mutt.

Disgust curled in his stomach. He couldn't show this pathetic man. It would disgrace him.

Another waste.

But no—he wasn't done with him yet. Maybe he still had talent. Maybe he was like an ugly duckling, and he'd have something else beautiful within. Dancing was clearly not his forte.

I've wasted too much time for you to not be worth it.

This guest proved to be another disappointment—no elegance, no grace. But not a complete lost cause. If he had him, he wouldn't let him go to waste.

"Forget it," he snapped. "Sit down."

The guest did as he was told, sitting quickly on the chair. He tried to speak through his gag, probably pleading for his life, but his words were unintelligible—and a waste of time.

He went over to the turntable and switched up the song, something more upbeat, more hoppity. Saxophones and trumpets blared from the speaker.

With his knife ready, he approached his guest, who once again, jittered in the chair. He placed the blade against his guest's throat, then carefully removed the gag.

Ah, time for his favorite part. If his guest could redeem himself this way—maybe he wouldn't be such a lost cause after all.

"Now," he whispered, *"sing."*

CHAPTER FOURTEEN

Cool, early morning air swept into Taylor's lungs as she breathed in, her feet pounding the pavement of a park just a block away from her home with Ben. A deep wash of purple swept over the sky, and the last of the stars faded as the sun began its ascent over the horizon. Taylor ran with her headphones blasting on full, wearing a loose black hoodie and leggings. It felt good to sweat. To put all of her energy—mental and physical—into keeping her legs moving, her breathing calm, her blood pumping.

Things at home were still tense with Ben. She hadn't told him about her visit to the tarot reader yesterday—her pride wouldn't allow it. Taylor could admit to herself it was her ego that stood in the way of her honesty sometimes; she didn't want to look like a fool after swearing all tarot was nonsense. Especially after what Belasco said last—that another death was coming. Taylor had tossed and turned all night in a fit of paranoia. And when paranoid thoughts took over, the rational mind left, and all that remained were the thoughts: *But what if it* is *real?*

This whole thing brought back memories Taylor had worked so hard to forget. Memories of her mid-twenties, before she met Ben. Back when she was with Jeremy.

Jeremy. His name hadn't crossed her mind in ages. She'd rather it didn't. But in remembering his name—his face—came a flood of other memories, all of which Taylor wished would wash away forever.

Taylor had started dating Jeremy Eggert, an aspiring firefighter, right when she was a junior agent. He was the type of guy who could light up any party, the type who would have been popular in high school. More like someone Angie would have dated, not someone who would have chosen Taylor.

But he did choose her. And he was persistent about it, too. Taylor had no idea when she agreed to their first date what they'd go through as a couple—and what she'd go through as a woman.

The truth was, Taylor had seen one tarot reader before Belasco. Back when she was with Jeremy, a week before the warehouse incident.

She'd been pregnant at the time. It was an accident. But one she had welcomed. Back then, she'd been more optimistic, certain that things would just 'work out' the way they were supposed to, so she wasn't so concerned about dying on the job or leaving behind a child. She just wanted a baby with a man she thought she loved. It seemed like the next logical step to take in her life.

Jeremy's sister, Amy, had wanted Taylor to get a reading done to find out more about their child. Taylor thought it was all a bunch of bullshit, but like with Ben only days ago, she'd begrudgingly agreed, maybe just to shut Amy up.

It had been a cold winter night. Amy had hurried Taylor through the snow, to a small shop in downtown Portland. Unlike Belasco's, this shop was less extravagant, and the reader barely seemed to believe her own bullshit. She wasn't as theatric as Belasco, who really played the character up.

Of course, Taylor had gotten the 'Death' card from that reader too. It didn't bother her at all at the time.

Until a week later, while at work, when she wound up in that warehouse, where she'd gained her first gunshot, right through the abdomen.

Taylor survived. But the life inside her didn't.

Harrowed by the memory, Taylor pulled herself back to the present and quickened her pace, as if going faster would help her outrun her thoughts—outrun her past. Still, tears burned her eyes. Sometimes, when she was alone with herself, she couldn't escape her own mind, no matter how fast she ran. The thoughts of regret pooled back in.

Maybe if she'd listened to the stupid fortune teller all those years ago, none of that would've happened. Maybe she and Jeremy would've had that baby.

And maybe if she listened to Madam Belasco *now,* she could prevent another young man from dying.

But what did Belasco's reading even mean? Sure, she had read the cards, but now Taylor was powerless to do anything about it. So, maybe there was another death coming. Her line of work was full of death. She still had nothing, no leads to go off over who may be killing those young men—or when he'd strike again.

Because he will *strike again.*

Taylor's thighs burned as she looped around a street lamp. The sun rose above the houses that surrounded the park. Just as she stopped to catch her breath, her phone vibrated in the pocket of her hoodie.

It was Calvin Scott.

Taylor's skin crawled with anticipation and unease. She answered quickly.

"This is Taylor Sage."

"Sage," Calvin said. "I'm sorry to do this again. Are you home?"

She stopped and checked her watch, catching her breath. 5:30 a.m. "I can be in five minutes. Why?"

"Good. I'm coming to pick you up."

Taylor's heart sank. This didn't sound good. "Why? What's going on?"

Calvin sighed into the phone. "We have another body."

***

Taylor was beginning to feel a like her life was glitching, and she would be doomed to view these scenes in public parks until the end of time. They were in a park only twenty minutes away from Pelican Beach. The morning sun had fully taken over, and clouds were drifting over the clear sky. Taylor and Calvin stood in front of the park bench, taking in a similar scene to the last several murders.

This time, the body of a young man—no older than twenty-six—was slumped on the bench. His throat had been slit, but the blood had been wiped away, leaving nothing but a wide, red gash across his clean-shaven neck. The dress was emerald green, mostly made of silk, but with intricate lacing along the waistline.

A definite Monet.

Taylor had never been particularly interested in dresses, but even she was starting to pick up on his signature marks. The victim's smile was taped back, but his head hung low, making him look sad no matter what angle he was viewed at.

"His name is Samuel Faraday," Calvin said. "Twenty-four. He worked at a burger place downtown. Real quiet guy, apparently, and he was the youngest of four siblings."

"Jesus," was all Taylor could think to say. "Any wife? Kids?"

"None. He lived with his parents fulltime."

"In other words, nothing like the previous victims."

"So far, no connection."

Once more, nothing in common, other than being young men in decent physical shape. They would have to look into it more. But the truth was, with each death, Taylor became more convinced that this killer was selecting young men at random.

In truth, Taylor was too stunned and sickened to take this in. The murders were occurring in such rapid succession that she barely had time to absorb the last before another fell on her doorstep.

I need air. She stepped back and scanned the scene. The park was blocked off by caution tape as cops stood around, waiting for forensics. Storm clouds began to roll in more menacingly, blanketing the world in gray. The smell of oncoming rain penetrated the air—forensics would need to move quickly before all the evidence was wiped away. Not that Taylor felt confident there would be any. The dress was surely a Monet, but each crime scene had yielded nothing in the form of DNA.

Not a damn thing pointed to who was doing this. It frustrated her to her core.

Like the previous parks, this one was relatively isolated, but still open to the public. A peaceful place where people probably went on early morning jogs, much like the park she'd been in earlier today. Unlike the park Jacob Gregory had been found in, there were no trees surrounding it, making it very open and exposed.

That spoke of a cockiness to her. At first, she'd assumed the killer had crept in through the forest before, but the footprint lead from Jacob's crime scene never went anywhere. And now, with this, she imagined he'd parked right in the parking lot and walked in willingly, confidently, like he knew he wouldn't be seen.

Perhaps that was why he'd been choosing these small towns. Unlike cities, it was rare for people to be up at all hours of the night, roaming around. He would be safely shielded by the night, safe enough to drag a dead body out in the open and set him up like… this.

Taylor stuffed her hands into her pockets before she sucked in her nerves and took a step closer to the scene. She could picture Samuel Faraday in his fast-food uniform, working an entry level job like any other kid. Like the previous victims, he was conventionally good-looking.

But seeing him like this, all limp and defiled, felt like it'd ripped any dignity he'd had away. His body had been left here like a forgotten child's toy.

Like a ragdoll.

The word resonated like a gunshot through her head.

Ragdoll.

Doll.

Taylor's heart thudded. It struck her like lightning: the reason why Brent St. Clair's child, playing with her doll, had stood out to her the other day. For whatever reason, she'd been unable to shake the image from her mind, but now, it all made sense.

Maybe Taylor had been looking at this all wrong. She'd been thinking the obsession with dresses was something to do with women, or maybe just love and romance, but what if it wasn't that at all?

Maybe they weren't men dressed as women.

Maybe they were men dressed as *dolls.*

"Shit, Scott," Taylor said, palms sweaty. "We need to get back to HQ now."

Calvin looked at her, brows pinched. "Why? What's going on?"

"I'll explain on the ride."

Taylor had worked enough cases in her life to know when the spark of an idea truly felt alive. This line of investigation could lead somewhere.

Hurrying across the park, to Calvin's car in the lot, Taylor slipped into the passenger seat and buckled in. Calvin got behind the wheel and slammed his door shut, immediately starting the car and moving in reverse.

"Wanna tell me what's going on, Sage?" he said.

Taylor took a breath, before she said, "Dolls."

Calvin lifted an eyebrow as he geared the car out of the parking lot. "Dolls?"

"Yes, Scott. What if the killer views his victims as dolls?"

But he didn't look convinced, just stayed silent, waiting for Taylor to go on. She was still building this theory herself, but continued, "Just think about it. The way the bodies have been left out, it's been almost mannequin-like. And the dresses and makeup; I was thinking before that it felt like some sort of twisted romance, but no, it's a different type of possession. Maybe he doesn't view these men as lovers. Maybe he views them as items."

Calvin drummed his fingers against the steering wheel, deep in thought. Taylor anticipated his reply, hoping she didn't sound completely unhinged. It made perfect sense to her, and if she was right, this could lead them down a completely new path. She wasn't ready to bring up what she'd considered at Belasco's reading yet—about "inheritance" and "expectations"—but if the killer did have some sort of familial complex, an obsession with dolls could fit that profile. Victims of childhood abuse often get stuck in the years of their trauma, unable to mentally leave that time in their lives. Taylor had seen it over and over again throughout her career. And sometimes, that trauma led to violent tendencies as adults, as they never learned to properly manage their emotions.

"I see your angle, Sage," Calvin said. "The fact that he kept them so clean—aside from the makeup—could be considered 'doll like' too. Yeah, let's look into it."

A thrill ran through Taylor's chest. She was grateful Calvin was willing to listen to her theory. This one could be big.

Now, she just needed to get back to headquarters and explore it.

CHAPTER FIFTEEN

Taylor's fingers clacked the keys of her laptop, set up next to Calvin at the table in the briefing room in Quantico. Since they arrived, they'd each been doing their own research, trying to find a way to connect these murders to anything involving dolls. So far, Taylor was working on compiling a list of doll shops in the area.

There was a surprising amount of them, from vintage porcelain dolls to more modern collectors. Taylor felt the dress gave off more of a modern look, so she paid closer mind to those results. Although as she clicked through the various websites, she discovered they were all women-owned.

On a notepad, she jotted down a list of names. Just because they were owned by women, didn't mean those women couldn't have sinister men in their lives.

"Here, check this out," Calvin said. Taylor turned away from her computer, and he showed her his screen, where he'd done an internet search of plastic, Barbie-style dolls. The images sent chills up Taylor's spine. They were often seen in silky dresses with lace and frills. It might have been a stretch, but they were potentially similar to Monet's work. Taylor hoped she wasn't just seeing what she *wanted* to see.

"I was trying to see if any specific era of dolls matched up with the dresses we're seeing in the killings," Calvin said. "The style seems to have gained popularity in the nineties, continuing into the aughts."

"I've been noticing the same thing," Taylor commented. "Not incredibly vintage, but not incredibly new, either." She drifted off, biting her lip. If the dress styles matched up with those popular in that era, what could that tell them about the killer? They already knew the Francois Monet dress was from the '90s. Forensics would give them the date of the latest one, too, but until then, Taylor was left to ponder.

If we're dealing with someone who played with dolls in the '90s and aughts, then we're probably looking at a younger perp.

Someone closer to my age.

She'd suspected before that the killer may be young, as he was just starting out. But she wasn't sure if the dresses meant anything. It could simply be a style preference. Taylor decided it was best to focus on something more tangible. She handed Calvin the notepad of names she'd compiled so far.

"Look into some of these shop owners," she said. "Tell me if you get anything. And don't forget to look into their husbands, if they have any. Or sons. I'll keep looking."

"You got it," Calvin said, and he started on his laptop.

Silence befell them as each agent worked on their own assignment. Taylor appreciated the quiet. Her thoughts were racing so fast, they threatened to trip over themselves—she didn't need useless conversation slowing her down. Although Calvin was much chattier than her previous partner, he was always quiet when it mattered most, letting the work take over. Taylor was starting to appreciate him as a fine agent, and a pretty decent partner.

Taylor had been through her share of partners in her career, mostly when she was younger. Jenkins stuck around the most, being her partner for almost five years. Transitioning into working without him was surprisingly easy, although she did miss his gruff exterior and critical mind. Before leaving Portland, they'd said goodbye to each other the way they'd spent most of their partnership—in silence. He'd nodded at her as she left the FBI headquarters in Oregon for the last time, and she'd nodded back. Although part of her had wanted to hug him, she didn't. In a weird way, she regretted that now; they might never see each other again.

Calvin spoke, cutting her reverie short. "I'm not seeing anything here, Sage. Half of these women are windowed or never married, and they all seem squeaky clean. A couple of them have sons, but they're all less than twenty years old, which doesn't seem like our guy."

Taylor nodded. "It seems rare for a man to own a doll shop." But as she was saying it, another result popped up on her computer, about an hour away from D.C. It was a doll shop by the name of Lester's Dollies. For some reason, reading the name, a chill whispered across Taylor's skin, up her arms, like a ghost breathing over her.

She couldn't explain the sensation, but she clicked on the website fast. A pink, frilly webpage spread across her screen, followed by eerie images of dead-faced dolls in dresses, both vintage and modern. Taylor blinked, and for a moment, she imagined the images of the victims as these dolls, their dead eyes boring into the camera like dollies themselves.

She inwardly cringed, before she clicked on the 'about' page. An image of a man with a catlike smile took over the screen, reminding her of an old Mad Hatter. Lester Gould. He was the owner of Lester's Dollies.

This one, she decided to look into herself.

Calvin must have noticed Taylor's change in expression, because he cut in with, "What's up, Sage?"

Taylor lifted a finger, asking him to be quiet. She didn't mean to be rude; she was just in work mode. Calvin obeyed with no complaints.

Taylor pulled up the FBI database and typed in Lester Gould's information, quickly yielding results. Rather than ask, Calvin slid his chair closer so he could see her screen.

A picture of Lester, looking like an embalmed corpse, appeared.

Lester Gould. Sixty-two. He had a long history of mental illness, spending much of his life in and out of institutions against his will. But these days, it was a lot harder to force somebody into confinement, so that may have been why he was out. But that wasn't all.

He also had a record of attempted assault.

"Shit," Taylor said, quickly jotting down the address of the shop.

Calvin was already standing up, slinging his suit jacket over his shoulder. "Ready for another road trip?"

***

It was late afternoon when Taylor and Calvin arrived in D.C. The warm wind breezed over Taylor's skin through the window of Calvin's car as he drove, and rough, graffiti-splattered walls passed by as they entered the end of town Lester's Dollies was located in. Scabby, disheveled people hung around in the alleyways. A bad feeling churned inside Taylor.

Calvin had been uncharacteristically quiet on the entire drive here, but Taylor thought nothing of it. Maybe he was feeling tired or overworked. Plus, she wasn't complaining; she preferred the silence. But then Calvin pulled up a side street, one that was clearly not on the GPS.

"Why are we going off route?" Taylor asked, looking around. They were on a quiet, deserted side street, surrounded by seemingly abandoned shops.

Calvin stopped next to the curb and put the car in park before he sighed. Suspicious, Taylor eyed him.

"What is it, Scott?" she pressed.

An apprehensive look was slapped across his face, increasing her anxiety. Whatever he had to say—she wanted him to just get on with it. They didn't have time for bullshit. A killer was out there.

Finally, Calvin said, "Before we go in, can we talk for a sec?"

Taylor tried to hide her annoyance. "Okay…"

This, again, was so unlike Agent Jenkins. Jenkins never wanted to 'talk' in his damn life, at least not with that tone of voice, which sounded more like a teenager about to break up with their significant other. Taylor wasn't sure she liked Calvin's tone, but she was willing to listen. He'd been a good partner so far. And it was clearly important to him.

A few pedestrians passed by the car, but quickly cleared away. After a beat, Calvin said, "Listen, I don't want you to take this the wrong way. I know you're an experienced agent, Sage. More experienced than me."

Taylor crossed her arms, waiting for the blow. Wherever he was going with this—it didn't sound good. She could take criticism, although she wasn't sure how much she loved taking it from someone less experienced—who also barely knew her.

"But the truth is," he went on, "I didn't like the way you took off on your own at Monet's house. It was reckless, and you could've been hurt. When we go into this next place, I need to know you won't do something stupid like that again."

Taylor paused, taking in Calvin's words—and she couldn't fight the flame of offense that ignited in her. She'd worked too damn hard to be treated like some fragile woman, and *stupid?* Who did he think he was talking to?

"Pardon me, Scott," she said, "but if I hadn't done that, we wouldn't have even found out about the fur trade. Besides, you're my partner, not my babysitter—if anything, I've proven myself several times in combat, so I don't appreciate being treated like a helpless woman."

Calvin heaved out a sigh, which irritated Taylor more. "Yeah, I'm not your babysitter, I'm your *partner,* Sage. That means we're equals, even if you are more experienced than me—which is only by a few years, by the way. I'm twenty-nine, and you're what, thirty-four? We're practically the same age."

"Yet here you are, acting like a child when all I did was make a call—the *right* call." Maybe that came out too harsh, but Taylor didn't care—he'd officially gotten under her skin.

Calvin didn't reply. Tension seeped into the car on the quiet street as cars slowly passed. Taylor's temper simmered as Calvin seemed to be deep in thought, rubbing his temples like he had a headache.

Then, he said, "You're right. I'm sorry."

Calmer now, Taylor uncrossed her arms. "Where is this coming from?"

"Here's the truth...," Shame took over his face, and he looked down at his hands, wiping them across his pants. "I had another partner before you. She was only a year younger than me, so I felt like I was the senior agent," Calvin paused. Sadness filled his blue eyes. "Her name was Lara Wilkins. She was an extremely small woman, which I admit, worried me. Don't take that the wrong way, I know how strong women can be. But I mean she was *small*-small, like five-foot-nothing small."

Taylor built an image of this person in her head. Taylor, herself, was only five-foot-three, and considered relatively small for a law enforcement officer, which had worked against her in the past, like when taller men had been able to escape her by running so damn fast with their long strides. But making up for it with strong combat skills had benefited her. Plus, her small stature had worked in her favor before, too—she was quiet, sneaky, and agile, which had given her the upper hand in stealth situations.

Sure, five-foot-nothing was tiny for an agent, but if properly trained, the girl should have been able to handle herself well. Though she had a bad feeling about where Calvin was going with this.

Taylor squared her shoulders, listening as he went on.

"We were working a case at an apartment building—some sort of drug bust, you know the type. Rumors about cocaine use and guns. But we suspected some sex trafficking was involved as well. That made it serious." Calvin ran his hand along his short brown hair. "These were real dirty guys, so, we should've been prepared. And I thought we were, but..."

A pause hung in the air. Memories of her own career ebbed through her mind—the times she hadn't truly been prepared. The times her own hubris had made her believe she was invincible.

Subconsciously, Taylor ran her hand over her abdomen. The place she'd once been shot. When she realized, she pulled away.

Calvin continued, "One of the suspects fled into the building. We chased him down, but somehow, we lost each other. She got outside first, into a back alley, where the perp had run. I was trying to get there as fast as I could, but…," his Adam's apple bobbed as he swallowed. "I was still in the stairwell of the apartment building when I heard a gunshot."

Taylor's stomach sank, the scene playing out like a movie in her head. A gunshot.

Like in the warehouse…

"She got shot, Sage," Calvin said, voice thick with regret, "and by the time I reached her, it was already too late. There was blood fucking everywhere. She was lying in a pool of it. She died on the scene—she was dead before I even got there. And if I'd just arrived faster, if I'd been her proper backup, she—"

"Scott, stop," Taylor cut in. She'd never been one to give pep talks, but Calvin, apparently, needed to hear this from someone. "It wasn't your fault," she said. "You can't think like that. Getting hurt is the risk we take when we become agents. You know that, and so did your partner."

Calvin's eyes were downcast, like he didn't believe it at all. "I know, but still. I wasn't there for her like I should've been."

Taylor sighed, her heart heavy. The truth was, no one had ever died under her supervision—she couldn't pretend to imagine the grief Calvin had to endure. Taylor was normally the one throwing herself at danger and getting hurt—but none of her colleagues had ever fallen on the same job as her. She was thankful for that every day.

She understood now why Calvin was so worried when she split away at Monet's. It must have brought back traumatic memories, but as much as Taylor would like to give him peace of mind, she wasn't a liar—she couldn't promise him it wouldn't happen again. She had to do her job the way she'd always done it, and hopefully, in time, he'd learn to appreciate that about her.

"I'm sorry you went through that, Scott," she said. "Really, I mean that. But you can trust me to take care of myself in the field. What happened to your partner is a tragedy, and I can't promise neither one of us will ever not get hurt on the job. But I'm going to trust you too. We'll have each other's backs, but we're federal agents—sometimes, that means we have to make a call in the moment. Sometimes, it won't be the right one. But sometimes, it will be."

A ghost of a smile crossed Calvin's lips. He nodded. "All right. You're right—I should trust you, it's just… hard when emotions get involved, you know?"

"I get it," Taylor said.

Calvin nodded. “Sorry, again. I was out of line.”

She almost smiled too. “Let’s just start fresh, okay? We’re going to be all right.”

“I hope so.” A disturbed look contorted his gentle features, and he ran his hands over the steering wheel, looking out into the empty street. “I have a gut feeling about this next guy—and it’s not good. When we go talk to him, we should be extra careful.”

As much as she appreciated Calvin opening up, they’d also wasted enough time talking. Time to get on the road. “You’re right, we should,” she said, “and we should also get moving.”

Wasting no more time, Calvin put the car in drive. They slowly crept up the street, as they were already close.

Things between them felt better now, and Taylor respected that he’d opened up about his past. It took strength, she realized, especially in a man, as most of the men she’d known—other than Ben and maybe her father—were socialized to keep their emotions locked in a tight box. But Calvin had taken a risk with her, and Taylor appreciated that. He wasn’t as immature as she’d thought, just flawed. *We all are.*

As Calvin turned up the next street, the sign for Lester’s Dollies appeared up ahead, and Taylor’s palms grew sweaty.

She had a bad gut feeling too. And with each passing second, it was only getting worse.

CHAPTER SIXTEEN

The shop towered above Taylor as she and Calvin stood outside. Its Lolita-esque sign, with its frills and curly letters, gave Taylor the creeps, and she peered at her partner in her periphery. She had one more thing to go over with him before they went in—and that was their approach. It would be easier if they had a game plan, especially if Calvin was still apprehensive about her making calls in the middle of the action.

"Scott, before we go in," Taylor said. They stood off to the side, just out of sight of the windows, in case the owner was looking through. "Let's take a different approach. You and I are having the same gut feeling that this could get ugly."

"You could say that," Calvin muttered, looking up at the store's sign with dread.

"Right. So let's pretend to be a couple shopping for our kid."

Calvin's eyebrows shot up. "Wow. Really?"

She shrugged. It was definitely unorthodox for her, but it'd been a long time since she'd had a partner close to her age. "Unless you have a better idea."

"No, I'm game," Calvin said. "Just didn't strike me as your style."

It wasn't, really. Other than the one time she and Jenkins had disguised themselves as father and daughter to get a farmer they suspected of murder to speak up. It had worked then, so maybe this would work now.

The door dinged as Taylor and Calvin entered. The smell of mothballs and damp wood irritated Taylor's nose. The lighting was fairly dark, most coming from the windows at the front, and dolls upon dolls were in boxes against the walls. Taylor couldn't help but think they all looked like little corpses, embalmed in their eternal coffins.

There were racks set up around the aisles, ranging from porcelain dolls to plastic. It looked like he had every kind imaginable, from every year on Earth—old dolls, plush dolls, Barbie dolls. He had them all.

"Shit, this is creepy," Calvin whispered.

"No kidding," Taylor muttered back.

The faint sound of music box-style tunes trickled through the air, along with Taylor and Calvin's footsteps, as they creaked over the hardwood floor and filled the narrow shop.

Then, as if out of thin air, a man appeared.

"Hello there!"

Taylor jolted, hand instinctively going toward her gun hidden under her jacket, but thankfully, she caught herself before she blew her cover. This place—this entire *case*—had her way too high strung. Forcing herself to relax, though still on guard, Taylor took in the man in front of her. If the shop was creepy—this guy made it look like nice. The picture on the website didn't do him justice.

Lester Gould was tall and lanky, with big, bug-like eyes that were so pale they were nearly gray. He appeared soulless, but he wore a Cheshire Cat smile, and wrinkles folded on his leathery skin. Wispy brown hair sat on top of his head, and he wore a button-up shirt with a tie and brown slacks.

"Uh, hi there, sir," Calvin said carefully.

"How can I help you kind young folks?" Lester's glassy gaze flicked between Taylor and Calvin. The bad gut feeling grew stronger, activating Taylor's adrenaline. *Could this be our killer?* But she had to keep it together.

"We're looking for a doll for our daughter," Taylor said. "We were wondering if you could help us."

"Wonderful! I would love to help!" Lester exclaimed. "You two are a lovely couple. How old is your daughter?"

Taylor and Calvin exchanged an uneasy glance, before Calvin blurted, "Uh, six."

"Six!" said Lester. "What a lovely age. So lovely and small. What kind of dollies does she like?"

"Well, we're not really sure," Taylor said, stepping over her words. "Maybe you can help us find the perfect one. She likes... dresses. With silk and frills." *Monet dresses.*

"Silk and frills? We have lots of that here. Just look around!" he chortled. "Well, your daughter is so young, but I bet she'd love a nice classic doll."

Lester hobbled over to a display case containing several porcelain dolls, each lit by its own light. Hesitantly, Taylor and Calvin followed. These were probably the expensive ones. Taylor wondered how he kept this place afloat. Did that many people really love dolls these days? It was hard to imagine.

"Do any of these girls speak to you?" Lester asked, and Taylor was undoubtedly disturbed by his use of the word 'girls.'

None of the dresses quite resembled a Monet. They were mostly lacy, old-fashioned, on dolls with perfect skin and rosebud lips. Another thing Taylor noticed was, none of them smiled—but that wasn't unusual on a doll. If Lester was their guy, maybe he liked that he could make his 'live dolls' smile himself.

Near the display case, there was a rack of small cars fit for plastic dolls. Calvin strolled over and picked one up. "Wow, these are neat," he said, "don't you think, honey?"

It took Taylor a moment to realize he was talking to her. It felt undoubtably weird for anyone other than Ben to call her *honey.* Snapping out of it, she nodded. This was certainly not the way she imagined her first time shopping for a child would be like, even if it was fake.

"They're great, aren't they?" Lester said.

"Very spacious inside." Calvin held the car up to his eye and peered through the tiny windows. "You could fit a few dolls in there, no problem."

"Oh, of course," Lester said with an uneasy laugh.

"What kind of ride do you have?" Calvin kept his tone casual and light as he put the car back down. "Maybe something with a big backseat? Lots of trunk space?"

Taylor understood where Calvin was going with this—he was trying to gain details that could lead them to a vehicle matching any of those seen in the area the night of the murders. But this likely wasn't the best approach.

"Uh, well, it gets me from point A to point B," said Lester, confusion in his voice.

Taylor gave Calvin a nod, as if telling him to leave it alone—this line of questioning could freak him out. And judging by his twitchy mannerisms, Lester was already starting to seem on edge. He definitely gave off a creepy aura, though with his frail arms, Taylor had a hard time seeing him haul athletic young men to park benches in the dead of night. But stranger things had happened.

Calvin put down the car and returned to Taylor's side, scanning the wall of dolls.

"What year are these from?" Taylor asked.

"Hmm, they all have a variety of ages, but these girls are bit older, from the early 1900s. But trust me, children love them just the same as a fancy new doll." He ran a finger over a case, but didn't touch it. "To be honest, sometimes it feels like they have their own souls, and each child who plays with them gets to bond with that soul. Generations of young souls, all bound by one doll. It's a nice thought, isn't it?"

More like creepy. A chill slithered up Taylor's spine. To be frank, they were quite old and dusty, and she had a hard time imagining kids these days, who were used to iPads and phones, being compelled by a toy such as this. And besides, when she was a little girl, being told her doll had a 'soul' probably would have given her nightmares. After all, she'd seen other kids destroy their dolls at school and on playdates.

This was starting to go nowhere fast. It was time to step this up a notch and gauge Lester's reaction.

"Not quite what I'm looking for," Taylor said. "I'm looking for more of, say, a Francois Monet?"

Lester lifted an eyebrow, hands shaky. "What's this?"

"A Francois Monet," Taylor doubled down. "Do you know him?"

"Well, he's no dollmaker," Lester said. "I know every dollmaker in the country, maybe even the world."

Taylor couldn't tell if he was bullshitting or not. Either way, she didn't trust him. But how could they get him to say something tangible, something that would actually prove his involvement?

The best thing she could do was crank it up a notch—and start to peel back why they were *really* there.

"Actually, to be honest, we're a bit put off by dolls," Taylor said, "but we'll do anything for our little girl."

"Put off?" Lester asked, offended. "What for?"

"Haven't you heard about the murders happening in the area?" Taylor asked. She took a moment to glance at Calvin, comforted by his presence near her, in case this guy got violent. A breath, and she continued, "The young men being laid out in parks wearing dresses. When I heard about the case, I couldn't help but think they reminded me of dolls."

That was probably too bold—but at this point, Taylor was ready to ramp things up. They didn't have time for more games. Lester was suspicious enough to warrant questioning—that was all she needed.

"What is this about?" he asked, taking a step back. His face twisted. "You two don't seem like a couple. You don't even like my dolls!" Lester's voice raised, becoming whiny and grating.

Shit. Taylor raised her hands in peace. "No, no, we love the dolls," she said, hoping she could save the moment. But it was too late. Lester's face contorted with rage.

"You asked for nice dolls," he ranted, "and that's what I have! Now you're asking about some other dollmaker I've never heard of? Are mine not good enough for you?!"

"Whoa, okay, calm down." Calvin lifted up his arms, just enough for his badge to flash—and Lester saw it. His eyes bugged out of his skull.

"Police?" he exclaimed. "You lied! You lied to me!" He backed into the aisle. *Fuck!* Taylor went to grab him, but Lester picked up a doll and swung it right at Calvin. It nearly hit him, but Calvin swiftly ducked. The doll collided with the display case. Then, the distinct shattering of porcelain all over the floor.

Taylor jumped back. Shards spilled all over the tile, followed by the corpse of the doll. Its face had been broken in. Lester gasped and fell to his knees, collapsing next to the doll.

"No, no...," He tried to scoop up the remains, avoiding the sharp edges. He held the limp body of the doll in his hands like a parent mourning their child.

It was an odd sight, seeing a grown man so distraught over an object. He ran his finger over the doll's cheek, and Taylor swore a tear welled up in his eyes.

A wave of guilt hit her. It occurred to her that they had no *proof* Lester was their guy. As he slumped on the ground, looking completely torn over a broken doll, she wondered if he'd even be capable of taking a life. Maybe he was just strange. Maybe he had a difficult childhood, and that was why he'd clung to these dolls.

She'd seen so much evil that nearly anything could be contorted into something twisted, something perverted. But Taylor had to consider that maybe Lester *was* just strange. Strange didn't equal evil.

She kneeled beside him. If he cut himself on that broken porcelain, it could be bad. She needed to bring him back to Earth.

"Mr. Gould, it's all right," Taylor said. "We just need to take you in for some questioning, okay? Will you come with us?"

Swiftly, Lester grabbed a jagged piece of porcelain, and in a flash, slashed it at Taylor.

It cut right through her jacket, down to her skin. The hot pain moved up her arm as she winced and retracted.

Calvin was there immediately, tackling Lester to the ground. He pressed his face against the tile as he read him his rights and cuffed him.

Taylor stood back, shocked, feeling the sharp pain move up her arm. But all she could do was focus on Lester, staring blankly at the broken, shattered doll. The only thing he seemed to care about.

CHAPTER SEVENTEEN

Taylor's arm still burned from the gash Lester had left on her. While Lester was handcuffed in the back of Calvin's car, Taylor and Calvin stood outside of the shop so they could make sure her wound was fine. Her sleeve was pulled up, and the afternoon sun only brightened the red on her pale skin.

"That looks rough," Calvin said. "We should get you to a hospital."

Taylor observed the wound, opening it slightly. It wasn't that deep, but she didn't want to show how much it stung. Thankfully, most of the bleeding had stopped. She'd definitely had much worse—but this was going to leave a scar.

"I'm fine," Taylor said. "It's barely bleeding."

"Hey, you made me go to the hospital when I was hurt," Calvin reasoned.

"Not happening, Scott. I'll clean it at the station." With that, Taylor rolled her torn-up sleeve back down. She glanced at Calvin's car, where Lester was.

On top of his creepiness the fact that he'd attacked her so suddenly and violently should have made Lester a viable candidate. However, as much as the gash hurt, it was superficial—hardly the handiwork of a seasoned murderer. Plus, he was so frail—Taylor couldn't picture him lifting a muscular young man's body over his shoulder and carrying it into a park, and there was no evidence at any of the scenes of a wheelbarrow, or any kind of transporting device being involved. There would have been evidence in the grass.

But maybe Calvin had a different idea, so Taylor asked, "What do you think about this guy?"

Calvin sighed, hands in the pockets of his pants. He glanced at the car and squinted in the sunlight. "Not much. He's unhinged, but physically weak. I took him down like a sheet of paper. Do you think he could even carry the bodies around?"

So, they were on the same page. Taylor looked through the tinted windows at the silhouette of the frail man trembling in the backseat of Calvin's car. Her gut had definitely warned her before that Lester could get violent—which he did. But now, it was telling her that, as unhinged as he was, he was maybe *too* unhinged to pull off this intricate series of crimes. But there was only one way to find out.

"C'mon," Taylor said, "we might as well question him now, while he's calm."

They approached the car and carefully opened the back door, where Lester could barely move with his hands cuffed.

"Can't move, can't move," he mumbled, but his thrashing had stopped. Instead, he solidified, like he'd been turned to stone. He had wide, buggy eyes like a patient trapped in a strait jacket.

"Mr. Gould, we're going to ask you a few questions now," Taylor said, crossing her arms, "and we'd appreciate it if you could stay calm."

Lester didn't reply. Calvin leaned against the open door of the car while Taylor kneeled down so Lester could see her, even though he refused to look. He'd gone completely still, but she began her usual line of questioning anyway.

"Mr. Gould, can you tell me where you were the night of Wednesday, July 14th?"

She waited. No response came.

"Mr. Gould," Taylor pressed. He still wore that dead stare, like he couldn't even hear her. She sighed. Maybe a more visual method would jog his memory. Removing a photo of Jacob—his graduation picture from university—from her pocket, she flashed it to Lester. "Do you recognize this man?"

Still no response. Taylor wagged the photo in front of Lester's eyes, but it was like they were made of glass. He couldn't even register the image in front of him, and a stream of drool leaked down the side of his mouth.

Taylor stood, frustrated, and tucked the photo away. She stuffed her hands in the pockets of her jacket. "He's gone completely catatonic," she said to Calvin. "This is useless."

Calvin sighed in exasperation and closed the back door, shutting Lester in again. He didn't even react. "This is going nowhere fast. Least we can get him for assaulting you, but…"

"We're no closer now than we were at the beginning." More frustration burned into Taylor. She stepped back from the car and paced across the sidewalk. They couldn't afford this. Not when another victim was probably being scooped up at that very moment. "Scott," Taylor said, "we're way too far behind the eight ball. We have a new body dropping daily. This is bad. Really bad."

"Trust me, I know." He ran his fingers through his hair, stressed. "But we have nothing, Sage. Gould led us to a fat nowhere. Unless you have any ideas, I think we're stuck at yet another dead-end."

Taylor brought her thumb to her mouth and bit down hard on the nail, a habit she'd mostly broken unless under extreme stress. Taylor had worked many cases in her career, but out of all of them, she'd never seen a timeline escalate so suddenly—and so fast. Daily victims were unacceptable, and if she didn't pick up the pace now, she figured she didn't even deserve to be called a federal agent. Maybe someone else would be better for the job, because lead after lead, idea after idea, was getting her nowhere.

She needed outside help. And while Calvin Scott was a decent partner, she wanted someone with more knowledge in psychology.

Calvin must have noticed Taylor's panic, because he stepped forward and attempted a reassuring smile. "Hey, we're doing our best. But there's nothing else we can do right now. Let's call it quits and regroup in the morning."

When we have another body? Taylor wanted to say, but she kept it in. Because she had a different plan now.

"All right," Taylor agreed. Although as usual, she had no intentions of calling it quits.

***

An aquarium bubbled on a desk by the wall, containing a multitude of colorful fish. Taylor watched as they swam, moving in their hive mind synchronism, as she sat on the green couch in the room at Quantico, waiting for the psychologist to show up.

Taylor had yet to meet Dr. Jarvis, Quantico's in-house shrink, and she was hoping she wouldn't have to. Psychologists tended to make her weary—she'd grown up as the daughter of one, after all. She adored her father and respected his work, but she also knew all about psychoanalyzing—and how psychologists tended to subconsciously do it to, well, everyone. It made her feel more under a microscope than in a safe space without judgement.

After a few more moments, Jarvis—a tall, slender woman with a bob haircut—strutted into the room, her movements agile and swift. "So sorry for having you wait, Agent Sage," she said and slid behind her desk, next to a bonsai tree.

Taylor nodded and forced a small smile. "No problem at all."

Dr. Jarvis clasped her hands on her desk, peering at Taylor from behind thick-rimmed glasses. She had cat eye makeup and a tiny mole beside her left eye. "You're new here, right? It's great to meet you. I've heard fantastic things."

Taylor's face warmed. She hadn't realized how many people would actually know her when she moved here. Sure, that case with the mother who'd tried to frame her husband was big, but she hadn't expected it to have spread so far.

"Thanks," she mumbled. "And likewise."

"So what can I do for you today?" Jarvis asked. "Should we start off by getting to know each other? I'm Dr. Cynthia Jarvis, and—"

"Actually," Taylor cut in, "we can skip that part. I'm here for a more specific reason."

Jarvis's eyebrows rose. "Oh? Go on, then."

Taylor took a breath, hoping Jarvis would take this well. "The truth is, I'm working an incredibly difficult case right now, and I feel like I keep hitting brick wall after brick wall. Every time I think I'm onto something, it ends up being nothing. Still… I can't help but feel I'm at the cusp of a breakthrough, but haven't quite penetrated the surface yet. I'm hoping someone with your expertise might be able to see something I'm missing."

Jarvis leaned back in her chair, taken aback. "Well… I'm happy to help in any way I can. You're on the dress case, yes? With the young men being staged?"

So, she was aware of the case. Taylor nodded.

"It sounds like this is taking quite the emotional toll on you," Jarvis said. "Why don't we start there?"

Taylor feared this would happen—that the shrink would try to make this all about Taylor's feelings, how the case was affecting her, etcetera. But Taylor didn't care about that. All she cared about was catching a killer, whatever the means.

So she ignored Jarvis's question and said, "I've been developing this theory, slowly but surely, about who the killer might be. Right now, I've settled on the idea that maybe he's acting out some sort of conflict with a parent, and that he may have an obsession with dolls. I'm thinking abuse, or overbearing expectations, may have led him to become sort of trapped in his childhood. Maybe trying to prove to his parents he can 'be' something, but that something is a serial killer."

Taylor left out the part where a fortune teller had given her the initial idea of it involving parents, considering she read her cards about inheritance and overbearing expectations. Taylor couldn't risk her professional reputation by letting her colleagues know she was, apparently, starting to think tarot wasn't all bullshit. Taylor could hardly face the fact herself, let alone take in what others might think.

Jarvis's brows pinched like she was deep in thought. "That's an interesting theory, Agent Sage. It compels me that you'd mention parenthood. Maybe you experienced something similar in your childhood—the 'overbearing expectations?'"

Taylor's teeth instinctively grit. She didn't come here to talk about the demons of her own childhood. Even though her parents were both loving and accepting people, she had experienced her own share of negative emotions associated with them, especially after Angie disappeared.

Dark times Taylor didn't wish to confront assaulted her mind. After Angie's disappearance, her parents had been in shock. Her mom cried almost every night, and her dad became more absent, burying himself in his work. Taylor remembered spending so many nights alone in her room, asking herself: *Why her, and not me?*

Her parents had raised both her and Angie to feel loved and accepted. When Angie was still around, Taylor never felt like either parent had a 'favorite,' although Taylor identified more with her dad, and Angie more with her mom.

Still, although Taylor never vocalized it, part of her fourteen-year-old mind had wondered if her parents would have been happier if *she'd* been the one to disappear instead of Angie. Sometimes Taylor even wished it herself. Angie had been a ray of light, while Taylor had always felt so bland; the household would have been brighter if the roles had been reversed.

As an adult, of course, she knew her parents never wanted that; they only wanted *both* of their daughters at home and safe. Her parents lost hope anything about Angie would ever be found. But Taylor still believed someone out there knew what happened to her.

She snapped herself from the memory, frustrated that Jarvis even got her thinking about her past. *Focus. Remember what you're really here for.*

"All due respect, Dr. Jarvis, but I didn't actually come for therapy," Taylor said. "I'm hoping you can help me psychoanalyze this killer."

Jarvis shifted uncomfortably in her chair. "I understand, but I'm afraid that just isn't my job here. I'm supposed to help agents process traumatic events they may encounter on the job and are difficult to live with. If you would like to talk about that, then…"

Taylor understood Jarvis's point, she really did. But with her situation, to be blunt, she simply didn't care. "Dr. Jarvis, I know you're doing your job. But I need you to understand that this case is escalating at an alarming rate, and I've gotten nowhere. If I don't get something going quick, I'm going to have another dead body tomorrow, another young life senselessly snuffed out." Taylor paused. She could see the discomfort all over Jarvis's face, but now wasn't the time for emotions. "If you really want to help me, please hear me out."

After a long, uncomfortable pause, Jarvis cleared her throat. She adjusted her glasses, lips pursed, and said, "All right, Agent Sage. If I can help, I will. But I'm not so sure I can."

Relief flowed through Taylor. "Great. If you don't mind, can I show you some photos?"

Grimly, Jarvis nodded. Taylor figured if she was an FBI shrink, she must have at least had some guts. Taylor kept the photos of the various crime scenes in her jacket pocket, and she placed them on Jarvis's desk for her to see.

"I can see why you want to get this dealt with quickly," Jarvis commented.

"I'm sorry for the imagery, but it's important."

"That's all right. I had heard some of the details of the case. These are not pretty." Jarvis squinted, eyes skating over the pictures. "I think you might be onto something with the familial theory … it's a very interesting concept, and I'd be curious to know how you came to the conclusion. However, I'm a bit more interested in the staging of the bodies."

"How do you mean?" Taylor leaned forward, intently listening.

"Well, they're so specific. It definitely seems as though the killer is sending a message—what that message is, I can't say. However, there is far too much pageantry here for this to be a mere amateur at what he does."

Pageantry.

The word hit Taylor like a brick over the head.

She'd thought about dolls. But pageants—that was a totally new angle, and she wanted to smack herself for not thinking about it sooner.

Taylor abruptly stood, startling Jarvis, and ran right out of the session. As she entered the hall, she took out her phone and called

Calvin. She hurried toward the briefing room, and finally, Calvin answered.

"Sage, what's going on?"

"You need to get back to HQ now," Taylor said, huffing as she caught her breath in the briefing room. "I have a new angle on this thing."

"Now? Sage—"

"Now, Scott," Taylor said, not liking that she even had to repeat herself.

But time was of the essence. If the killer stuck to his current timeline, then chances were, he already had his next victim.

And maybe this time, if she acted quickly, Taylor could save a life.

CHAPTER EIGHTEEN

His hands relaxed on the steering wheel as he drove smoothly through the night. The road was bumpy, and rocks occasionally popped up from beneath the wheels to *ting* against the metallic body of the car. A starry sky spread above, the waxing moon emanating rings through wispy clouds.

"Isn't it pretty?" he mused, but no response came. In the rearview mirror, his latest guest was sound asleep in the backseat, head back and mouth ajar. Such a pretty man. Mother would like this one. He was sure of it this time.

He drummed his fingers against the wheel and hummed a soft show tune, then continued, "Pretty nights like this always bring me right back. To nights under the tire swing, swinging away under the big oak tree. I thought if I swung high enough, I could reach the stars..."

He sighed wistfully, reliving the memory.

"Mother could be strict sometimes," he went on. "I remember she would get so mad if I were out too late. But she just wanted what was best for me, I know that now. Do you have any little ones? Maybe you know what it's like."

Still no reply. The car moved over a bump in the road, and the guest shifted positions in the backseat, although he still hadn't woken. What a surprise he was in for when he did.

Breathing in deeply, happily, he rolled up to his home, where he had spent all of his life playing and growing. His guest didn't realize what an honor it was to be here, surrounded by these fields, all this history. The tire swing still hung from the old oak, illuminated by the starlight, backdropped by an acre of farmland he'd stopped tending to long ago. The silvery moon made the untamed grass look like a million tiny blades.

After he parked the car, he stepped into the warm night and stretched his limbs before he went to the back door and popped it open. Unbuckling his guest's seatbelt, he lifted his lithe, but athletic frame with ease. It was a good frame—not too big or bulky or ugly. Mother had always wished he'd been smaller and slimmer, a dainty flower like her. But this man would do.

He dragged his unconscious guest up to the deck, where the porchlight clicked on. After unlocking the door with a free hand, he shimmied inside, his guest's feet dragging the whole time.

"Mother, are you awake?" he called into the house. It was dark and quiet, a thin film of dust over the surfaces of antique clocks and tables, but this was no classless, old-school farmhouse. Mother had taken care of it well. The vintage, yet posh furniture was home to him.

He flicked on the light in the living room, still hauling his guest. A smile curled at his lips as he observed the rocking chair.

"There you are, Mother," he said. "I have a surprise for you. This one, I think you're really gonna like. I know the other men I've brought back were inadequate, just like me, but I have a great feeling about this one."

Mother didn't reply, just kept on rocking, but that was okay; she'd see soon enough.

"This time, I'll get it right," he said before pulling his guest toward the workshop door across from the living room. The guest's foot dragged over Mother's best Basquiat rug.

The workshop was his safe space. And he'd already picked out the perfect dress, so excited to have this guest tonight. This perfect guest who would surely please Mother once he was all dolled up.

He put him in the room, where he had his chair and rope set up, waiting, next to his makeup kit. The dress, a beautiful, royal purple, hung on a hook by the door. He pulled his guest into the room and laid him on the concrete floor, before he picked up the dress. Maybe that was what he'd done wrong before. Maybe he needed his guest to wear the dress *first,* before the fun began.

Forcing a man's limbs into a dress wasn't always a graceful sight, and it was harder when the man was still alive. He was grateful Mother would only see the final product. After stuffing his guest's boyish body into the beautiful gown, he dragged him onto the chair and bound his chest to the back, making sure his hands were safely secured as well. The last thing he needed was a tussle to ruin this moment.

He took a step back to survey his work. The light dangled over his guest's head, illuminating the lovely tones of the purple on the man's creamy white skin. Perfect. Now, all he needed was his makeup.

Just as he was about to pick up his kit, his guest's eyes popped open, terrified.

A smile graced his lips as his guest took in the room, his circumstances. And the man before him.

Good. Now, the true fun began.

CHAPTER NINETEEN

Taylor waited at the table in the briefing room with her laptop open, tapping her fingers anxiously against the wood. Calvin was supposed to be there any minute, but Taylor hadn't wasted any time diving into her latest theory, compliments of Dr. Jarvis.

Beauty pageants.

The webpage in front of her contained many images of young women in dresses, and it was about the history of pageants, specifically in the D.C. area. Some images were more vintage, black and white photos from the '30s and '40s, but as she scrolled down the page, more color came to life in the beautiful women with extravagant hair and makeup. And when she started getting to the '80s and '90s, the dresses began to take a familiar shape.

Lace and silk.

Taylor's heart pounded as she opened a new tab and typed 'Francois Monet' and 'beauty pageant,' while silently cursing herself for not thinking of this before.

The first article made her stomach drop, her palms clammy. It read:

"Seventeen-year-old Holly Burwell wins beauty queen award, sporting a custom Francois Monet dress."

Holy shit.

Taylor clicked the article. They'd done some research into Monet's clientele before, but obviously, they hadn't gotten to this. And that irritated Taylor even more. Every case, she learned something new about herself as an agent, and hindsight was always 20/20, but she still chastised herself for not seeing this sooner.

She was about to read the article when the door to the briefing room opened and Calvin hurried in. Taylor could smell the patchouli cologne on him. A look of hurried disappointment was on his face, and he'd shaved his jaw clean.

Clearly, she'd interrupted something.

"All right, what's going on?" He slid into the chair across the desk. He was wearing a clean black sweater and a nice watch. "I hope this is important, Sage."

Taylor couldn't help but be annoyed. Important would be an understatement. "What, did I interrupt a date?"

"If you have to know, yes, I did have a first date with someone, but—"

"It is important," Taylor cut in, not actually caring what Calvin was doing. They were agents. When work called, saving lives was more important than whatever they had going on in their own personal lives. Sometimes, that meant having to sacrifice making other people happy.

Taylor thought of Ben, alone at the house they'd just moved into, the house she'd barely been in. A fleeting moment of guilt struck her, but she pushed it aside—this theory was too strong to sleep on, especially with evidence that Monet was linked to the beauty queen world.

"I have a new theory on our killer," Taylor said, "and we need to move quickly. Like I said earlier, the timeline suggests he may already have his next victim."

Calvin leaned back in the chair, hands behind his head, clearly trying to seem present. "Okay, let's hear it."

Taylor flipped her laptop toward him. Calvin leaned forward, brows pinched as he read the webpage she had open. Taylor watched intently, waiting for him to get to the part that would register.

And it did. Calvin said, "Holy shit. Monet dresses."

"That's right," Taylor said. "It seems they have a history in beauty pageants. I don't know how we missed it before, but here we are."

"But what does it mean?" Calvin asked. "You think we have a beauty queen killer? Enacting revenge on guys who remind of her an ex-boyfriend or something along those lines?"

"Not exactly." Taylor leaned back in her chair and crossed her arms tight over her chest. "Given the pageantry of the staging, plus the dresses, I do think the killer could be connected to the world of beauty pageants—but I don't think they're a participant themselves. What I'm saying is, I still think the killer is a man, but maybe his mother is the connection to pageants."

Which would tie into Taylor's earlier theory, too, that there was some sort of familial link. *Overbearing expectations.* A profile was building in her mind, begging to take shape, now more than ever. She was still missing pieces, but she was close.

"Well, I can't deny what I'm seeing here," Calvin said. From his laptop bag, he pulled out his laptop. "Where should we start?"

Taylor took her own laptop back and readied her fingers on the keyboard. "I'm not exactly sure what we're looking for, but let's start by finding pageants in the area, from small towns to D.C." Something told her they'd know when they found it.

"All right," Calvin breathed out. "I'm on it."

She could tell he wasn't thrilled to be working instead of courting some girl, but he was still there, still reliable. Taylor shot him a rare—and quick—smile. "Thanks, Scott. For coming in."

He smiled back. After that, only the sound of their keyboards clacking filled the room.

On her notepad, Taylor jotted some of her research. Apparently, Monet dresses were fairly common in the pageant world, and many different beauty queens from children to teens had chosen to wear his gowns in their competitions. In recent years, though, his popularity had died down.

Guess that's why he switched to selling illegal furs, Taylor thought grimly.

She found a couple of places where Monet dresses were more common, all female-owned. She wrote down the names of each woman with plans to investigate their histories and if they had any sons or husbands. It might be like trying to find a needle in a haystack, but Taylor would bleed every lead dry if she had to.

After doing some further research, Taylor stumbled upon a training agency called *Winning Princess.* Just as she was about to look into them, Chief Winchester stormed into the room. He looked like he'd aged a year since the last time Taylor saw him. He'd been around HQ, but busy with other tasks and had barely checked in on Taylor and Calvin's progress. But the harried look on his face didn't tell Taylor good news.

"Special Agent Sage, Agent Scott," Winchester said, voice gruff. "I see you two are busy."

"Trying, sir," Taylor said, sensing his sarcasm. Sitting around looked bad, and Winchester knew how many leads they'd exhausted with no real progress. Taylor hated feeling incompetent—but this time, she was onto something. She had to be.

"Good," Winchester said. With an exasperated sigh, he crossed his arms over his wide chest. "We're getting word that the murders are hurting tourism in the area. This is highly problematic for the local economy, since so many of these small towns rely on tourists coming in and wasting money. You know what I'm saying, right?"

"Sir—" Taylor began, but Winchester cut her off.

"Capital's on my ass about this. You two need to shut this guy down—and shut him down fast."

"But—" Calvin began, but Winchester sliced in again.

"I don't want excuses. I want results. I'll be checking in tomorrow. Get to work."

With that, he breezed out of the room, letting the door slam behind him.

"What does he think we're doing?" Calvin muttered, annoyance in his tone.

For a moment, Taylor felt hollow. This was her first case at this location, and her superior already wasn't impressed. This wasn't at all how she'd wanted to start things off at Quantico—but she couldn't let that distract her.

"He doesn't care what we're doing," Taylor said. "He only cares that we've been on this case for days, we've lost three new victims, and we still don't have a concrete lead." She refocused on the laptop, pushing her feelings of incompetence aside. "So let's hurry this up."

Calvin didn't look pleased, but he kept working anyway.

First, Taylor started vetting her list of pageant owners. One woman, Mary-Beth Egerton, had a son. Taylor was able to access the database to find him.

Jordan Egerton, twenty-six.

But he lived in Scotland. *Great.*

And the rest of the list yielded even more useless results. Most women had daughters, some no children at all. Some were married, but their husbands came up squeaky clean—either that, or they were dead.

Just as Taylor felt she'd reached another dead end, she remembered that she never checked into the owner of the training agency before Winchester had interrupted. She went back onto the internet search to dig in. Its full name was *Winning Princesses Professional Pageant Training Agency,* and Taylor clicked on the website.

It was simple, yet elegant, with a blue and gold theme and a serif font, no flashy graphics. On the "about" page was an extensive history, reading:

Winning Princesses Training Agency began more than three decades ago, started on a dream—a dream by an eight-time pageant winning queen Brandy Johansson.

In her teens and twenties, Brandy's love for pageantry rocketed her to local stardom. Her talent in dancing, singing, art, and of course, her winning smile, made her known as a beauty queen extraordinaire—a true force to be reckoned with.

But Ms. Brandy's dream didn't end with her winning pageants herself. No, she wished to pass down her gifts to other girls, so they could also achieve their own dreams of being a beauty queen. That was when she chased her dream of owning her own agency and founded Winning Princesses.

At Winning Princesses, we know that pageants aren't won with beauty alone. Our students are talented, diligent workers, go-getters who will stop at nothing to achieve their dreams.

Do you have a winning princess?

If this sounds like you—or your child—please contact us for a private consultation.

All of that seemed completely normal, but as Taylor finished reading the article, the fine print at the bottom caught her eye:

Ms. Brandy is now retired, but her dream continues. The agency is now run by her loving son, Mark.

The feeling—like she was actually getting somewhere—returned to Taylor in full force.

Quickly, she went into the search bar and looked up Mark. A quick search showed his full name was Mark Johansson, and he'd been running the business for ten years now, since he was thirty-eight years old.

With bated breath, Taylor opened up the FBI database and typed in Mark's information. The page loaded, and Taylor's heart pounded.

A mugshot appeared, showing a pale-faced man with sunken cheeks and empty gray eyes.

Mark Johansson wasn't just a simple pageant trainer.

He also had a record of assault.

She slammed her laptop shut and stood, slinging her jacket over her shoulder, startling Calvin from his work.

"I've got someone," Taylor said. "Come on. I'm driving."

CHAPTER TWENTY

Taylor shivered beneath her jacket under the dusky sky as she trekked down the sidewalk. Despite the summer heat, a chill flowed through the air as she and Calvin approached an old building that had been converted into a studio. It was two stories tall, all red brick, with chimneys and pipes that went out of service back when this was a factory. Above the building's roof, the setting sun cast an orange smear over the cool blue sky.

Winning Princesses was in the heart of D.C., on a quiet back road in a gentrified industrial neighborhood, and it said it would be open until eight p.m. It was already seven now. Taylor, naturally, had not been willing to wait until the next day to investigate, so she and Calvin had gotten on the road immediately, with Taylor behind the wheel.

Now, a bad feeling churned in Taylor's gut. The sign for Winning Princesses was displayed on top of a black door, and Taylor and Calvin entered in silence, prepared for anything after what happened with the last "person of interest."

The studio felt modern and open, with dim lights and exposed brick walls. A pretty young secretary sat behind a round desk.

"Good evening," the young woman said. "Are you here to pick up your little girl?"

Instantly, Taylor's jaw clenched. She wasn't sure why the question made her so on edge. Maybe the implication that she and Calvin were a couple, or maybe because the mention of her and children in the same sentence always made her uneasy. She tried not to show it, and before she could say anything, Calvin said, "No, actually, we're here to speak to the owner."

"Oh, not a problem at all!" the girl exclaimed. "Wait here, I'll be right back."

She zipped away, behind the wall that was erected past the desk. Through the gap in the walls, Taylor could see another room where little girls were dancing like ballerinas with a tall, lithe instructor. Then, she glanced at Calvin, who innocently peered around at the art on the walls like he didn't know what else to do.

Taylor pictured her and Ben coming to a place like this. Coming to *really* pick up their child. It seemed like such an impossible, faraway life. Taylor did want kids someday, but that 'someday' seemed to get further away the more it grew closer for Ben. He wanted to start a family *now.* But the timing never seemed right.

More guilt struck her. Had she sold Ben a lie by moving to Pelican Beach, by telling him things would be different here? Maybe she still wasn't ready. She'd felt closer to it before, but especially after seeing the aftermath of Brent St. Clair's life—the little girl he left behind—Taylor had been struggling to envision her own happy ending. The only thing that scared her more than dying on the job was dying on the job and leaving loved ones to pick up the pieces.

Just as Taylor was sinking into a deeper hole, a woman in her late thirties emerged from behind the wall as the receptionist scurried back to her desk to answer a phone call. Taylor and Calvin exchanged a confused glance. The owner was supposed to be Mark Johansson, a man, not this woman.

"Hi there," the woman said. She had a Southern twang to her voice, and she was as elegantly beautiful as the women Taylor had seen online. With her tall, slender frame and naturally delicate features, Taylor wondered if she'd ever been a beauty queen herself.

But she wasn't who Taylor had been expecting, and though she was disappointed to see her instead of Mark, she figured they should ask some questions anyway.

"Hi there," Taylor said. "It's nice to meet you."

"Of course, you too! I'm Erin," the woman said, "and I'd be happy to answer any and all questions."

Taylor hesitated. "We saw online that the agency is run by a Mark Johansson?"

"That's right, I'm his wife," Erin winked. "He likes to give me the night shifts. But I'm sort of the face to know around here anyway."

His wife—of course. Maybe she could be even more useful than anticipated. And it didn't surprise Taylor that the husband wasn't around. In fact, if he was the killer, and operating on the same timeline, with a new victim each night, then that would mean he already had his next victim.

"Where is your husband, then?" Taylor asked, trying to hide the urgency in her voice.

"Oh, he's around here somewhere."

Her chest dropped. Wait—he was *here?* "Oh, he's in the building?" Taylor asked.

"Mm-hmm!" Erin chirped. "His office, probably. He's been working his buns off in there all day. My Mark is very passionate about paperwork."

Taylor wanted to press more, but for now, it was probably best to play along and gain information gradually. If Mark was here—and he was the killer—then at the very least, the victim would be safe, wherever he was, for now.

But it doesn't add up. If he can be accounted for the entire time since the last murder, then he can't be our guy, not if he's operating on the same timeline.

"C'mon, let me give you a tour!" Erin waved her hand for them to follow, and so they did, moving through the open concept studio. As they passed through to a stage area, a rack of dresses was set up along the wall. Taylor took a quick glance.

Lace and silk.

Monet.

Her palms grew sweaty as she glanced at Erin's back. She was wearing a form-fitting black dress. When Erin turned back with a warm smile, Taylor's eyes darted away.

"So, are you two parents?" Erin asked. "Are you hoping to enroll your little girl? You know, I used to be a pageant queen myself, and this agency trained me right up to be a winner. I speak from personal experience—our agency is the best at turning ordinary little girls into winning princesses," Erin winked again.

"Er, not exactly," Taylor said, walking alongside Calvin.

"Actually, we're with the FBI," Calvin interjected. "I'm Agent Scott, and this is my partner, Special Agent Sage."

Erin stopped in her tracks and faced them, wide-eyed with a theatric flair. "The FBI? Did something happen?"

Taylor and Calvin exchanged a knowing glance. They'd decided on the ride up to take an upfront approach and gauge reactions, rather than try to pull off any sneaky plays.

So Taylor said, "We're investigating a series of crimes," thinking it was best to leave out the specifics for now. "And we saw online that your agency has purchased dresses by Francois Monet before."

That last part was a lie—there hadn't actually been anything on Monet on the website. But Taylor was certain those dresses she'd just seen had been his handiwork.

"Did y'all see that online?" Erin frowned, perplexed. "I thought I got them to remove that… well, anywho, yes, Francois Monet has been the sole dressmaker for our agency since long before I was around. Since we opened, I'm pretty sure. Mark's mother is a big fan. She's the founder of this joint."

His mother... interesting, Taylor thought.

"So why remove him from your site?" she asked.

"Well, if you're with the FBI, and you're asking about him…," Erin's brown eyes darted around. "I'm sure you heard about the *allegations* against Mr. Monet. We thought it best to distance ourselves, as, you know, we have a very young clientele…"

"You mean about the teenage girl," Taylor clarified.

"That's right. We still have a bunch of his dresses, and I personally would like to get rid of him, but it's Mark's call." Erin cleared her throat. "Might I ask what you two are investigating? Did Francois get himself in trouble again?"

"It's actually a little more serious than that," Taylor said. "We're investigating a string of homicides that have occurred in some small towns surrounding the D.C. area."

Erin's jaw dropped. She was definitely a drama queen, Taylor could tell, but there was something kind and charming about her as well. She asked, "It wouldn't happen to be those men in dresses, would it?"

Taken aback, Taylor didn't respond. She knew the news was starting to spread, hence Winchester's outburst earlier, but the fact that Erin brought it up still caught her off guard.

"Yes, it is," Calvin said, sounding equally as surprised. "But what made you think that?"

"Oh, dear," Erin hugged herself tightly. "I've been hearing all about it on the news and Facebook. I heard it's real gruesome, serial killer work, you know, a little more intense than the odd shooting, which we're used to around here. My husband even knew one of the victims."

Taylor's blood ran cold, hands shaky with anticipation. Calvin, equally as shocked, shifted his weight beside Taylor.

"You *knew* one of the victims?" Taylor asked.

"I didn't," Erin said. "My husband did. He wanted to get him to enroll his little girl in our agency."

Taylor and Calvin looked at each other, a silent communication that said this was about to get real. The only one of the victims who had a child was Brent St. Clair and his daughter, Katie.

Something from their interview with Brent's wife, Annie, resurfaced in Taylor's mind. Annie mentioned Brent had an 'acquaintance' who was a professional in dealing with child models. Models… not pageants. But could Annie have just mixed the two worlds up?

Taylor's pulse drummed, and she refocused on Erin.

"Would that victim happen to be Brent St. Clair?" she asked.

"Hmm, Brent… that sounds about right. Yeah, his name was Brent."

"How did they know each other?" Taylor pressed.

"I'm not sure, really. Just acquaintances, I think. They weren't friends, really…"

Taylor swallowed the lump in her throat, tingly with anticipation. "Erin, would you happen to know where your husband has been for the last three nights?"

Now Erin seemed to catch on, her eyes nervously darting between the two agents. "What do you mean? My husband isn't a suspect, is he?"

"No," Taylor said, "we're just looking into everyone connected to Francois Monet. The fact that your husband knew a victim seems worth questioning. He isn't in any trouble. But please, answer the question."

Erin didn't reply, nervously fidgeting with the rings on her fingers. "Well…"

"Remember that we'll be able to find out, either way," Calvin added in with a kind voice, somehow making it feel like it wasn't a threat even though it very much was.

Erin nodded with a gulp. "The timing's a bit bad, unfortunately… because I can't say where Mark's truly been the last few nights. We got in a fight earlier this week, and he took off on one of his 'night drives.' He's taken one every night since, and I'm always in bed at midnight sharp… he's there when I wake up in the morning, but I couldn't tell you when he got home."

No alibi. Holy shit.

"Are these 'night drives' unusual for him?" Taylor asked.

"No, they aren't," Erin said. "He's done them our whole marriage. He says it's to clear his mind."

"Right," Taylor said. "That's good to know. Thank you. Do you—"

Taylor was about to ask where Mark's office was, as this was more than enough of a reason to take him in—but Erin cut her off.

"He'd never hurt anybody," she stammered with big, guilty eyes. "Not a chance, so—"

Just as Erin was about to finish her sentence, a tall, thin man with perfect posture strode up to them, wearing a casual suit. Taylor recognized him immediately, although he looked livelier now than he had in his deadpan mugshot.

Mark Johansson.

"Erin, what's going on?" he asked, warily eyeing Taylor and Calvin like he could smell they were cops.

"These fine agents just had a few questions, honey," Erin said sweetly. "Agents Scott and Sage, this is my husband—"

"You didn't think to wait for me before speaking to them?" Mark asked, nose high.

"I didn't think you'd be around!" Erin exclaimed, flabbergasted, and Taylor immediately got the vibe of what type of husband Mark was—the controlling type. Often, these personalities were equipped with narcissism and rage.

More rarely, homicidal tendencies.

The last one, she intended to find out.

"Mark Johansson," Taylor said, "we need you to come down to the station."

"Why? What is this about?"

"We just have a few questions for you," Taylor said, glancing into the room beside them that still had a group of little girls dancing. "We think the station would be a more appropriate setting."

After the last few perps, Taylor braced herself for a fight. A sudden violent outburst. But Mark didn't look scared. In fact, it was more agitation that crossed his features, like going to the station was an inconvenience to him. Like he wasn't worried at all.

Calm as ever, Mark simply said, "Fine then. Let's go."

CHAPTER TWENTY ONE

Taylor waited outside of the interrogation room with Calvin at the station in D.C. Through the one-way window, Mark Johansson sat alone at the table, looking agitated, but not frightened. Taylor couldn't tell if his cavalier attitude was indicative of his guilt—or his innocence.

"Think he's our guy?" Calvin asked, also studying Mark.

Taylor pursed her lips, eyeing their perp. "I don't know. He seems more inconvenienced than worried he's a homicide suspect."

She opened the file they'd dug up containing everything the government was aware Mark had ever done and flipped through the pages. There was one assault, where he had allegedly attacked a pageant judge a few years back, and a second assault—a violent outburst at a bar, where he was charged, but settled with the victim quickly and quietly.

Most importantly was, his whereabouts on the night Jacob Gregory, Brent St. Clair, and Samuel Faraday—the most recent three victims—still couldn't be confirmed.

Mark looked promising. Taylor prayed this wouldn't be another dead end. Suspect after suspect, and she'd grown tired.

But something still itched at her, and that was the thought she'd had back at the training agency—about the killer and his timeline. Taylor felt it in her gut that another victim had already been taken, and Erin could confirm that Mark was around all morning and all day. It frustrated her—for the first time in this case, it felt like every star was aligning. Mark had no alibi. He had a connection to one of the victims, and to the dressmaker. He was the perfect candidate.

So why didn't Taylor feel like justice was about to be served?

There was only one way to find out. No more wasting time. "We better go over our gameplan," she said, closing the file.

She was thinking it might be good to switch things up a bit. Thus far, she'd been taking the lead during interviews, but she couldn't deny that Calvin had a way with people—something about his empathetic voice and youthful appearance seemed to make people feel at ease. Taylor had noticed it before. She knew that she, herself, could sometimes come off as too blunt, even unapproachable. Calvin had proven himself skilled at interviews. Taylor wanted to see how he could handle being the one in charge, and if he could do 'bad cop' as well as he did 'good cop.'

"I've been thinking," Taylor continued, "why don't you take the lead on this one? Play a little bad cop?"

Calvin looked at her, brows raised in surprise. "Yeah? You sure?"

"Of course." Taylor almost smiled. "You've proven yourself worthy, Scott. I can sit back for this one."

Calvin grinned. "Thanks, Sage. Appreciate it. I know exactly where I can start." He gestured to the door leading into the interrogation room. "Shall we?"

With a nod, Taylor put on her good cop face, and they entered into the room. Mark looked up at them, still with annoyance on his features. He was an unassuming man, not particularly frail, but not in great shape either. He had a strong air of arrogance about him.

"And that took so long because?" he asked.

"I'm sorry, Mr. Johansson," Calvin said, sitting in his chair, "did you have somewhere important to be?"

"Funny," Mark muttered, arms crossed in a childish manner for a man pushing fifty.

Taylor slid into the seat beside Calvin and spread her portfolio out, ready to take notes. Calvin shuffled forward in his chair and cleared his throat.

"So, Mark. How did you know Brent St. Clair?"

Starting off strong. Taylor liked that.

But Mark just avoided eye-contact and said, "I have no idea who that is. Can someone please tell me what this is about? I had plans tonight."

Taylor and Calvin exchanged a look. Warning bells immediately went off—right off the bat, Johansson was lying. Erin had confirmed Mark knew Brent. But Calvin didn't call it out, not yet. Taylor watched intently, curious to see where he'd go from here.

"Mr. Johansson, where were you on Wednesday, Thursday, and Friday nights?"

"At home with my wife," he replied bluntly.

"But your wife mentioned you went out on a 'night drive,'" Calvin said.

"For a few hours. So what? I like driving at night. It clears my head."

"Where exactly did you go?" Calvin asked. "I need to know the time you left, and any stops you may have made."

"I didn't make any stops. I just left around 11:30 at night and got home closer to one. Ask my wife, she knows I wasn't gone long."

"Your wife couldn't confirm how long you had been out of the house. Maybe if you can give us any specific roads you may have gone down, we can dig up surveillance to confirm if your vehicle was spotted there."

Mark, shifty-eyed, leaned back in the chair and crossed his arms. "Okay, what is this about? Why would you need to *confirm* where I was driving?" Taylor and Calvin both looked at him, unblinking, until Mark just sighed and said, "Okay then. I drove through Bethesda and into the outskirts."

After jotting that down, Taylor observed Mark. He was beginning to grow fidgety, shifting around on his seat and tugging at the neck of his shirt. Telltale signs of anxiety—this was starting to get to him. Even sociopaths weren't completely immune to their subconscious body movements.

"We'll look into that," Calvin said. Switching gears, he kept his posture firm and went on, "Why don't you tell us about the assault charge involving a pageant judge on your record?"

"What *assault charge?"* Mark said in a mocking voice.

Again, both Taylor and Calvin glared at him in a way that said *don't waste our time—or else.*

So Mark, nose raised, said, "It was a misunderstanding. You have no idea what these judges can be like. He wrongly scored one of our girls and slandered our agency in the same breath. It was unacceptable. And he threw the first punch."

"Not according to your record," Calvin said. "In fact, it said you jumped over the judge's table to attack him."

Mark's arms tightened over his chest. He waved his hand dismissively. "Semantics."

Calvin glanced at Taylor and nearly rolled his eyes. She remained silent, but smirked, enjoying watching his interviewing skills. He was handling it calmly, coolly, and getting just enough information (and lies) out of Mark to implicate him.

"Anything else we should know about?" Calvin asked. "Any other charges?"

"No," Mark said sternly.

Calvin heaved out a sigh and leaned back in his chair, arms crossed behind his head. Then, he leaned forward and clasped his hands on the table, looking Mark dead in the eyes.

"The thing is, Mark, you've now lied to us four times."

Mark's eyes flashed. "I didn't lie."

But now he was starting to sweat, beads pooling on his forehead and gleaming in the dull light of the interrogation room.

"You had a second assault charge on your record," Calvin said, "when you just told us you only had one. Did you really think we couldn't find out everything about you?"

"Another misunderstanding," he stuttered.

"Furthermore," Calvin continued, "you knew Brent St. Clair—he was a potential client you were trying to scope out. And you also know he was murdered."

Mark went pale. "Wait… you mean *that* Brent? I didn't know his last name, I—"

"Your wife seemed to know his last name. She's seen it on the news and on social media. But you somehow missed it, even though—according to your wife—he was *your* acquaintance, not hers."

Calvin leaned forward, eyes intent on Mark. Mark shimmied back in the chair. His arms twitched like he wanted to get up and run.

There it was: the fear Taylor had been waiting for.

"It's interesting, Mark," Calvin said, "how you knew Brent St. Clair, who happened to be found dead in a dress by Francois Monet, the sole dressmaker for *your* agency."

Mark blinked. "I did not know that. I mean—I knew a dress was involved, but Monet—" His voice began to shake, panicky. "Monet was my mother's choice. To be honest, I find his work somewhat tacky. I would've switched dressmakers long ago if my mother hadn't loved him so much."

"Four men in total have been found dead in Monet dresses, Mark," Calvin said. His eyes became steely—a look Taylor had never seen on him. "Don't you think it's a strange coincidence, that you'd know someone who was killed and dressed up in a dress from *your* agency?"

The reality of Mark's situation seemed to settle in, and he pressed his palms on the table. He opened his mouth to speak, but only sounds stuttered out, before he managed to say: "Lawyer."

"Are you sure about that?" Calvin pressed. "Because—"

"Lawyer!" Mark exclaimed.

With a sigh, Calvin stood. Taylor slammed shut her portfolio and stood too, glaring at a now-shaking Mark. "That's fine," Calvin said. "We have all we need. Wait here. You'll get your lawyer."

As far as interrogations went, it had been a success. Calvin had done a great job getting Mark to crack, and asking for a lawyer either signified guilt or an innocent man who knew he was in deep shit anyway.

And everything pointed right at Mark. By all means, Taylor should have been thrilled to finally have the right man, to know she'd saved more lives from being lost.

But the timeline slithered back into her mind. Why would the killer start on such a rapid timeline—three murders in three days—and then just stop? Sure, Mark had no alibi for the nights of the murders, but he did have an alibi for the entire stretch of time since the last murder.

So maybe it's not him. Is it even possible?

Why can't I shake this feeling?

Calvin adjusted his suit jacket as he and Taylor left the room. And Taylor knew what she had to do next.

She just hoped the others would listen.

***

Taylor and Calvin were seated at the table in the briefing room, and Taylor couldn't get rid of the anxious ball in her gut. She had to tell everyone her theory—that Mark Johansson wasn't their guy—but this wasn't going to go over well, and she knew that.

Suddenly, Chief Winchester stormed into the room with a boisterous energy. "Great work, agents!" he exclaimed, extending a hand to Calvin, who stood and shook it.

"Thanks, Chief," Calvin said.

Winchester also offered Taylor a hand, which she stood and shook, albeit limply. But Winchester didn't notice, just crossed his arms proudly over his chest and clean suit.

"Johansson's in there with his lawyer, going over his rights, but this is a solid case," Winchester said. "I just watched the tape of the interrogation. That was excellent work, Agent Scott."

"Thanks, Chief," Calvin said, rubbing the back of the neck. "But this investigation would've been nothing without Agent Sage."

"Of course." Winchester's wise eyes fell on Taylor. "Sage, I heard you took the lead on the pageant angle. That was some excellent detective work. I had a strong feeling about you, given your track record. I'm happy to see I was right."

More anxiety grew inside Taylor. Winchester and Calvin stared at her, waiting for her to reply, to take in the praise—but she couldn't do it.

"Chief, I'm sorry," she blurted, then glanced at Calvin, "and to you too, Scott. Your interview was good, really good. But I don't think we should react so quickly. Mark Johansson—I don't think he's our guy."

A cold silence befell the room. Everyone blinked at Taylor, and she wanted to shrink into herself. Then, Winchester let out a hearty laugh.

"Agent Sage, I didn't know you had a sense of humor!"

"I'm not joking, sir," Taylor said, fists balled at her sides.

The smile melted off Winchester's face. And Calvin looked at Taylor with a confused scowl.

"Sage, what do you mean?" Calvin asked. "Everything's pointing to Johansson. We might not have anything physical yet, but the circumstantial evidence alone is enough to look into him. Once we get a warrant, we'll dig up all his dirt."

"It's the timeline," Taylor blurted. "Johansson doesn't have an alibi for the last three murders. But if the killer's moving on the same timeline, then that would mean he's been grabbing his next victims quickly. Which doesn't add up, because Johansson's wife can account for him since the last body dropped."

"Sage," Winchester said, "it's a valid enough point, but we've got the perfect suspect in custody. We're gonna get him. You can stop now."

"But what if I'm right?" Taylor asked, a hopefulness in her voice that they would just believe her. Believe *in* her.

This isn't over. I know it.

But neither Winchester, nor Calvin, looked convinced.

"Isn't it worth looking into more?" Taylor asked. "Even on the off chance?"

"I'm sorry, Sage," Winchester said, "but you're gonna need a stronger case than that. I told you before, we're on high pressure from the higher ups to book someone for this shit. And Mark Johansson is perfect. He's connected to both a victim and the dressmaker. We'll get the warrant to search his properties tomorrow, and I'm sure we'll find the physical evidence we need."

"But that won't matter if someone else dies!" Taylor exclaimed. Embarrassment warmed her cheeks at her emotional outburst. More silence in the room, before she went on, calmer, "Tomorrow isn't good enough. If the real killer is out there, and he has another victim, that means someone else will die *tonight.*"

"Sage, there's nothing else to say on the matter," Winchester said, voice stern. "We have our guy. Let it rest."

Taylor turned to Calvin, as if pleading with him to have her back. But remorse was written on his face. *He doesn't believe me either.*

"I'm sorry, Sage." Calvin gently grabbed her arm. She stiffened at the touch, but didn't pull away. With kind blue eyes, he said, "I've gotta get home and get some sleep. Maybe I can still catch my date. We did a great job today. *You* did a great job today."

"Scott..."

Taylor couldn't help but feel betrayed. She'd built respect for Calvin, and had even started to trust him. And her trust wasn't an easy thing to gain.

But he wouldn't even *entertain* the idea that she was right?

She shrugged away from his touch and hugged herself, looking away, feeling foolish.

"Sorry, Sage," Calvin said again, before he followed Winchester out of the room.

The door closed behind them, leaving Taylor alone. She was frustrated, and honestly, a little hurt. But as much as it stung and embarrassed her to not be taken seriously, maybe she was better off without them anyway. Maybe, this was a blessing in disguise.

Stifling her emotions, Taylor grabbed her laptop bag and left. Her work was far from over.

CHAPTER TWENTY TWO

Sitting in her office at home, Taylor tapped her pen against the desk and stared blankly at an empty computer screen.

She had no idea where to start looking into the next suspect.

The office around her, which was in the basement, had been mostly unpacked by Ben as Taylor had worked the case. It barely resembled her basement/office back at their old house, which had helped Taylor through some of her most difficult cases. Just the furniture was the same. But unlike her old place, which had its own dedicated room, she was sitting right next to the furnace and laundry machines, which she definitely didn't love. They'd remodel a room down here eventually, but until then, this was the most private spot in the house for Taylor to be. Maybe the change of environment was part of why her brain wasn't currently working.

Winchester and Calvin had a point—if their guy wasn't Mark Johansson, then who the hell was he? And was the pageant angle still relevant?

Taylor was certain it was. Especially with the Monet dresses, it was all leading somewhere, but where?

Could one of the clients be a place to start? But even if she went through a list of names of clients, how could she know which ones to zero in on?

Taylor's head spun. Damn her intuition. If it wasn't so strong, maybe she'd just be able to accept that Mark was their guy. But she couldn't. Not with this gut feeling clawing through her.

Then, suddenly, a voice ended her train of thought.

"Honey."

It was Ben. She hadn't noticed him come down. Hesitantly, Taylor swiveled in her chair and met Ben's apprehensive gaze.

When she had gotten home, Taylor briefly filled Ben in on the case, skimping on details, before she told him she needed to work more and locked herself in the basement. She could tell he wasn't happy, but she couldn't afford to think about it.

Not that she'd accomplished anything just sitting here, staring at her computer.

Stuffing that down, she forced herself to meet Ben's eyes. She couldn't help but feel guilty just looking at him. She wasn't being a good wife. But sometimes, she couldn't be both a good wife and a good agent. Sometimes, she had to choose. She'd thought Ben understood that, but it was proving to be untrue.

"Ben," Taylor said, "I'm sorry, but I really am busy…"

Ben sighed and put his hands on his hips. "Busy? Taylor, you arrested somebody today. You've been working nonstop. Why can't you just let this rest, even for one night, to spend some time in our new home with me?"

Disappointment and exasperation were all over his face, and Taylor didn't blame him. "Ben, I—"

"I've unpacked almost everything all by myself," he cut her off, "and you haven't even asked if I'm nervous to start my new job on Monday. Which I am, by the way, not that you care."

His petty attitude was rubbing her the wrong way, but Taylor decided not to comment on it—she didn't want this to escalate into a fight, even though Ben was clearly looking for one.

"I don't understand," Taylor said calmly. "You used to give me space when I needed to work. You know this is serious, Ben."

"Yes, but we both agreed that when we moved here, we moved here for a reason. For you to start your new job, and maybe decrease your workload so we could start a family." He threw his arms up. "This big house with all these rooms isn't for just us, Taylor."

She understood what he was getting at, and her stomach curled. "I can't talk about this right now, Ben."

"Then tell me what's going on."

A burst of emotion struck her. She stood and approached him, hoping if she saw him eye-to-eye, he would understand what she was going through. Because it was a lot of stress, a lot of turmoil—so much that she kept in, and Ben didn't do much to comfort her either.

"If you have to know," she said, eyes stinging, "the man we arrested today—I don't think he's the right person. And I'm terrified—*terrified*—that another one has been taken, and the real killer is out there, free to torture whoever he wants. Do you have any idea what that burden feels like?"

Maybe it was naïve, but Taylor hoped Ben would understand, would see her side through his anger. But her husband's breathing only became more ragged, more irritated.

"No," he said, "I don't. And I'm sorry, but I don't get the sense you've arrested the wrong person. I think it's more likely you're running again, just like you did before. You can't stand the idea of not working, so you're beating a dead horse. Just admit it: you're scared of trying for a baby."

Taylor flinched at the coldness of her husband's words.

A couple of years ago, back in Portland, when Ben was softer about her work, he'd asked for them to try for a baby. Taylor had agreed, even though it terrified her then, too. She'd always known she wanted children someday, but ever since what happened when she was younger, she'd been scared. And her work was so important to her. She couldn't imagine ever not being an FBI agent. She also couldn't imagine dying on the job and leaving a child to grow up without a mother.

An event Taylor didn't like to think much about weaved its way into her mind. It was a cold night in February, and Taylor's period had been late by nearly a week. She hadn't told Ben yet. He was standing in the kitchen of their old house, having a late-night cup of coffee as he stared out the window, at the snowflakes slowly falling.

Taylor approached him, her body shaking. She hadn't bought the pregnancy test yet—they'd tried one the month before, and she'd been secretly relieved that it came back negative. But this time, with her period being late, she feared it would be positive. And she wasn't ready to face that yet.

The whole situation had suddenly become incredibly real. When Ben had noticed her in the kitchen with him, he turned to her with a warm, loving smile, one full of innocence and hope. Recalling the memory, Taylor realized that she hadn't seen that on him in a while.

"Hi, honey," Ben had said, going to embrace her.

But she had gone stiff beneath him. "Ben, I have to tell you something…"

"What is it?" He touched her chin and tipped her jaw upward, forcing her to meet his kind and loving eyes. "Good news? Are we finally—"

"My period is late," Taylor blurted, backing out of his touch. By that point, Ben must have realized something was wrong, because he looked at her with brows knitted in concern.

"Honey, that's amazing," he said. "What's wrong?"

"No, it's—it's not amazing," she stuttered. "Not at all."

"Taylor, I—"

"I don't want this, Ben," she said. "I don't. I can't. I'm not ready."

She began shaking, tears threatening her eyes. A look of confusion—and a bit of offense—crossed Ben's face. But Taylor didn't care. Everything was falling on her head, and she wanted nothing more than to run away.

"Taylor, you're not thinking clearly," Ben had said. *"Of course* you want a baby. We've talked about it a billion times."

"No, I'm not ready," she said. "Ben, I can't give up my job. My life. My career. I'll be pregnant for months, and I won't be able to work, and—"

"Shh," he cooed. He stepped forward and gently touched her arms. "Taylor, it's okay. We're in this together, remember?"

"But what if we do have a baby, and I get hurt at work? What if I never come home? What if—"

"We can't worry about that. And if things get too dangerous, well… I can work, and you can stay home."

A feeling of offense had burned through Taylor. She hadn't worked so hard to become an agent just to be typecast as a housewife. Of course, she wanted to have kids someday, and that meant the risk of her keeping her dangerous job to do it. Not working had never been an option. It wasn't that Taylor never wanted children; she just wasn't ready *then.*

"No—I've made up my mind," she'd said. "I'm not having a baby. I'm *not."*

"But if you're already pregnant—"

Taylor, with anxiety crippling her, stormed away. She couldn't talk to Ben about this. She needed to be alone, so she hurried through the snow and into her car, driving to the nearest motel.

She barely remembered sleeping that night. But in the morning, with the sunlight through the windows, she woke up delirious in the motel, like she'd been pulled from a bad dream. And she was given a gift: her period.

The relief she'd felt was unparalleled. She wasn't pregnant. And calming down from the terror of her anxiety attack, she returned home to a heartbroken Ben. He'd hugged her and said, "It's okay, my love. We can wait until you're ready."

Two years later, barely months ago, they made the plan to move to Pelican Beach. They had decided that, now, Taylor was closer to being ready. Soon, they would try for a baby. *Soon.*

But this case she was working, although only a few days out so far, had awoken so many memories in her, and maybe Ben was right—maybe she was still scared. But she *did* want a child. She wanted to raise somebody who could be a good person in such an evil world, and make a positive difference.

"I *do* want to have a baby," Taylor said, leaving out the 'but.'

"I don't know if I believe you," Ben said. "You always have excuses. You never want to try. We haven't even had sex in two weeks, and—" He stopped himself.

Hurt, Taylor hugged herself. She didn't like this either.

"Forget it," Ben muttered. "I'm going out. Don't wait up."

With that, he turned and stormed up the stairs.

Taylor watched his retreating figure as he disappeared and slammed the door behind him, shaking the house. *I should go after him,* she thought, but something in her stopped her.

And that something was that the killer was still out there.

Ben was hurt, but he would be okay. Whoever the next victim was wouldn't be able to say the same thing. So, as much as it hurt her, Taylor locked her fight with Ben into a box. She would deal with it later.

For now: the case.

There was something she was missing about it, and someone else she still hadn't visited to talk about it. Taylor's father lived only a thirty-minute drive away in Baltimore—it was one of the benefits of moving over here. Growing up, he'd been her hero, and in that moment, she felt like she needed him more than ever.

She dialed her father's number, and within three rings, his familiar voice flowed through the phone. Relief washed over her. Nothing brought her back to the innocence of her childhood like her father's voice.

"Taylor?" her dad said.

"Hi, Dad," Taylor smiled into the phone, feeling emotional. "Any chance you're up for a visitor?"

CHAPTER TWENTY THREE

When Taylor arrived at her parents' house, the smell of maple syrup and cooking pancakes wafted into her nose, despite the fact that it was now pushing 9:30 p.m. and the sun had set. Taylor's heart warmed—it had always been her dad's tradition to make her pancakes, no matter the time of day, whenever she was upset. She didn't realize how much she needed this.

Taking off her jacket, Taylor hung it on the coat hanger. Her parents had a cottage-like home, but with tall ceilings and an open concept living room. Various themed artwork hung on the wooden walls, and the house had a musty, yet comforting smell. Taylor felt *home.*

"Taylor? Is that you?" her mother called out. She trotted down the stairs to the foyer, wearing a black, flowy dress with glasses with beads around the neck. Her once-brown hair was now a tasteful gray, and she hurried up to Taylor, trapping her in a hug before she had a chance to

"Hi, Mom," Taylor mumbled.

"Your father just told me you were coming. Where's Ben? Is he not here?" Her mom's eyes were intense. She'd always loved Ben and had been the number one advocate of their marriage. Taylor didn't know how to tell her that she and Ben were on rocky terms. That didn't mean their marriage was in trouble, of course—they could definitely survive this. But Taylor wouldn't be able to put energy into him until she caught this killer.

"Just me, Mom," she said. "Actually, I'm here to see Dad. It's sort of work-related."

"Well, that explains the pancakes for dinner," she muttered, then patted Taylor lovingly on the arm. "All right then, I'll go back to my studio. You two have a good talk, okay?"

"Thanks, Mom."

Taylor's mom went back upstairs, then into the garage, where her art studio was set up. Taylor went up the stairs until she found the kitchen, where her dad, Randall, was flipping pancakes in a patterned cardigan. Like her mom, age had turned his hair a light gray.

"Dad?" Taylor said, and he looked over his shoulder with a smile.

“There you are, kiddo! I didn’t hear you come in.” He flipped a finished pancake onto a plate next to the gas stove he was working at.

“You didn’t have to do all this,” Taylor said, approaching the kitchen table. “It’s pretty late for pancakes, don’t you think?”

“I could tell something was up on the phone.” He flipped the last pancake onto the plate and turned to Taylor, bringing two heaping plates of pancakes to the table and setting them down. “Wanna talk about it, kiddo?”

She sat down at the table. She definitely didn’t want to talk about what had her spirits so low, which would be the fight with Ben. “No… but there is something else.”

Her dad sat down and slid her plate in front of her, as in telling her she was eating whether she liked it or not. The warm, sweet smell of banana filled her nostrils, and her mouth watered. She realized then that she’d barely eaten today.

Pouring maple syrup over his pancakes, Taylor’s dad said, “How can I help? I’m all ears.”

Taylor took the syrup as well, pouring a light drizzle over the banana pancakes, before she limply cut a slice off, but didn’t eat. “I’m working a case right now, and I’m stuck. You’ve probably seen it on the news. The men being found in dresses.”

Her dad’s face went grim. “Oh, yeah, I saw that one. Truly wretched stuff. I didn’t realize you were working it—you haven’t checked in much since you moved, and I assumed you and Ben were busy unpacking.”

“Ben has been. I’ve been working nonstop,” Taylor paused, poking at her food. “We made an arrest today.”

“That’s fantastic, sweetheart,” her dad said, mouth full of pancakes. Hesitantly, Taylor took a bite as well, comforted by the familiar taste of her dad’s cooking. Her dad went on, “So what’s the issue?”

Taylor put down her fork. “The issue is that I’m not convinced this is our guy. And no one at work believes me.” The fire burned in Taylor again, overpowering her melancholy feelings. “Dad, the killer has been dropping a new body every day. I’ve never seen such a rapid timeline. The guy we arrested today can’t be accounted for the nights of the murders, but—if he’s operating on the same timeline—then that would mean he already has a victim. And he can be accounted for all morning and day since the last body dropped.” Frustration burned through her. “But my colleagues at the FBI seem to think it’s more important to bag someone so we can move on.”

Her dad's eyes flashed. He'd always believed in Taylor, in her gut instincts and feelings. He was always her number one supporter of becoming an agent.

"Sweetheart," he said, "if you're convinced that he's not it, then you have every right to keep looking. Forget if your colleagues don't believe you. *You're* the brilliant mind on this case." He dropped his utensils, clasping his hands on the table. Then, suddenly, his eyes became downcast. "Ever since what happened to your sister, you've questioned everything. In a good way."

Discomfort radiated through Taylor. Her dad didn't bring Angie up much.

"My point is," her dad went on, "I raised a brilliant agent. So if you think the killer is still out there, I'm inclined to believe you."

Taylor smiled. The first real smile in a while. "Thanks, Dad."

"Now, enough of that," he said, putting his authoritative voice back on. "Tell me about the case. What are we dealing with here?"

Taylor pulled out the photos, which were tucked in her bag, and tossed them across the table. Her dad kept eating a pancake like it didn't faze him as he looked at them.

"The first guy was found last year," Taylor said. "Last three, all within the last three days."

"Yikes." Her dad slid the photos back, and Taylor tucked them away.

"It's not pretty," Taylor said. "I've run through a lot of theories, interviewed a lot of people, most of which have gone nowhere. But I haven't been able to shake the idea that there's something maternal about this case, but it's not just about the mother."

"Maternal… interesting," her dad said, stroking his hand over his clean-shaven jaw.

"What are your first thoughts?" Taylor inquired, leaning forward intently. She loved picking her dad's brain.

"Well, for one, I see shame here. It's something in the messiness of the makeup, and even the men dressed as women themselves. I see self-hatred. After all, he's killing men, not women. And we can rightfully assume this killer is a man."

Taylor nodded. As always, her dad had a keen eye. "Right. I ran through a few ideas—lovers, dolls, etcetera—but I think you're right on the mark. It *is* self-hatred."

"True psychopathy is rare," her dad said. "It's much more likely for evil to be *made.* With the level of hatred and shame we're seeing in these crimes, the killer was likely a victim of childhood abuse himself."

"I've been thinking the same thing."

"Right," her dad said. "Given that, if you can narrow down something to search through the department of children and families' files, you might have something to run with."

DCFs. Of course! If there had been any reported child abuse, it would be in the system. As for cross referencing names, Taylor knew exactly where to start.

In a hurry, she whipped out her laptop from her laptop bag and put it on the table, opening it in a flash.

Her dad sighed, "Hey, I know you're busy, kid, but don't forget to eat."

Taylor grabbed a pancake with her hand and took a bite as she typed into the keyboard. "Thanks, Dad."

He chuckled warmly before he got up, his own plate now empty. "I'll let you work. Let me know if you need anything."

Taylor didn't reply, as her vision was now zeroed in on the laptop.

In a few quick strokes within the database, Taylor accessed the DCF files on families in the D.C. area. It was going to take some digging, but maybe—just maybe—she could find a promising list of Winning Princesses' past clients and do a cross-reference. If she was lucky, a name would match up.

Specifically, she searched Mark Johansson's mother Brandy's past client list, and began accumulating a list, jotting down each name in her notebook. There were a good number of articles, and by the time Taylor was done with her first round, she had thirty names. There were more out there—but this was a start. For her own sanity, she organized the list into alphabetical order, by last name, to coincide with the DCF files. Each article was also accompanied by a photo of the pageant queen—immortalized on the internet for all to see how beautiful they were.

With that, Taylor scrolled through each respective list. A had no matches. From B to F, nothing.

Please tell me I'm not wasting more time.

Under J, there were two Johnsons who had once attended Winning Princesses: Mary and Agnes. There was a near endless supply of Johnsons under the DCF files—and four Marys. The spark returned, giving Taylor hope. Mary Johnson was a common name—but one of these women could be who she was looking for.

She slogged through cross referencing them. But not a single Mary Johnson from the DCF files was the same Mary Johnson from Winning Princesses.

Not a single match.

"Damn it!" Taylor shouted, instinctively shoving away from the table.

"Taylor, are you all right, honey?" her mother called from somewhere in the house.

Regaining her composure, Taylor fixed herself at the kitchen table. "Fine, Mom!" she shouted so her parents wouldn't worry themselves. Frustrated, she picked up a pancake and took another bite, although they'd grown soggy and cold.

This wasn't over yet—she still had the rest of the alphabet to work through. She continued down the list. But by the time she reached Q, she was losing hope. There were only so many letters left.

On R, Taylor found nothing.

But on S, the last name Swanson appeared a few times. And the name Matilda Swanson appeared on each list—the DCF files, and the list of Winning Princesses's clients.

Taylor had to look twice. There were definitely two Matilda Swansons—and that was a much less common name than Mary.

So she dared to keep her hope alive as she dug into it. On the DCF side, Matilda Swanson had been reported to child protective services. The file had a photo of her. And when Taylor went into the article on Winning Princesses's Matilda Swanson, she saw two images of the same woman.

She was a steely-eyed beauty, and her timeless brown eyes bored into the camera, as if looking through Taylor's soul. Despite being an esteemed beauty queen, Matilda's smile, unlike many other pageant girls, did not reach her eyes. It was a feigned joy that Taylor could see through. A hollowness.

This could be her woman.

The DCF file stated that Matilda was investigated twenty-five years ago. She lived on a farm outside of D.C. Her husband, the owner of the farm, had passed away years prior, leaving the farm to her.

And she had a son, Jeremiah Swanson.

When Jeremiah was a in the fourth grade, a teacher alleged she saw bruises on him and reported Matilda to authorities, suspecting abuse. However, without sufficient evidence, the case was dismissed.

Matilda then pulled Jeremiah from school. As far as the file said, Jeremiah never went to school again.

If that were true, that would leave him with the proper education of a fourth grader, even into adulthood. Who knows what Matilda may have homeschooled him with? He may have never mentally advanced beyond that age if not properly educated. And if the abuse was real, then Jeremiah would have been trapped in his own hell for all of those years.

The next step was to look into Jeremiah himself. The database had no records of any arrests—on paper, he looked clean. However, he was listed under welfare, and had been admitted into a hospital once after an alleged suicide attempt. He had never been able to hold down a job, and though he still lived in that same farmhouse, it hadn't been operational since his father died. The property had been fully paid for, so all Jeremiah needed was to keep the lights on. Matilda, in her old age, had a retirement fund set up and money left behind from her husband.

But that wasn't all Taylor found.

Matilda Swanson had been diagnosed with cancer. And the date that her official diagnosis was put on her file was one week before the first victim, Frank Turner, was found dead.

Taylor's heart began to battle her ribcage. Her hands shook as she continued down the page, leading up to Matilda's fate.

It was just as Taylor had suspected.

Matilda Swanson had died three days before the killer resurfaced.

CHAPTER TWENTY FOUR

Taylor peeled out of her parents' house and dove for her car, parked behind her dad's SUV in the driveway. She dialed Calvin's number as she ran. It beeped several times in her ear. She slid into the driver's seat as it went to voicemail, and she left the following message:

"Scott, call me back ASAP. We have the wrong guy." She started the car and backed out of her parents' driveway, continuing, "His name is Jeremiah Swanson—I'm driving to his house right now. The address is 599 Constitution Road, just outside of Glenview. His mother was a client of Winning Princesses's—and she'd been reported for child abuse. Jeremiah never recovered. Scott, it's him. I need you on this one."

Taylor's voice came out more pleading than she realized, but she needed Calvin to believe in her. According to her GPS, she could arrive at the Swansons' farmhouse within twenty minutes. She didn't have time to wait for backup—Swanson already had his next victim. She was sure of it.

Her hands were shaky on the wheel as she made her way through Baltimore, then into thc outskirts of town. The light pollution slowly bled away from the sky, where the emerging stars beamed through. A full moon hung above like a giant eye, watching her, and Taylor felt an ominous chill in the wind.

This wasn't another dead end. Taylor felt it throughout every fiber of her being.

She just prayed Calvin would get her message in time.

***

A long, dirt road, lined by trees, led Taylor to a quiet and secluded farmhouse. She parked the car a good distance away to give herself a moment to prepare. Still no word from Calvin. A pickup truck was parked outside, and the lights were on in the house.

Taylor's nerves were on fire. She took a moment to calm down, taking in the scene before her. The full moon soaked the farm in its silvery light. A large oak tree grew on the lawn facing an overgrown field, and a tire swing slowly swayed in the gentle nighttime breeze. There was a dilapidated barn in the distance, and the field beyond the fence had overgrown grass sprouting up in every direction.

Cows likely once grazed there. Taylor saw flashes of a different time, back when this was a lively export of local goods. But like the file said, the farm hadn't been operational since Edgar Swanson—Jeremiah's father—died.

All these years, Matilda and Jeremiah had lived here. Jeremiah, isolated from the world, forced to grow up on a non-operational farm with no friends from school. Taylor could easily imagine what that type of childhood could do to a person.

But did that give him a right to do what he'd been doing? Absolutely not. And that was why Taylor was here to take him down.

At the same time, she knew that this time, she was dealing with the real thing. And she was still alone. She checked her phone once more—no word from Calvin. Taylor inhaled a shaky breath and shut her eyes. Her gun was holstered safely beneath her coat, but she was dressed like a normal civilian. She needed to plan this out.

Her best approach was probably to be soft. Ease into the questions, make Jeremiah feel safe. She could be a reporter asking about his mother, doing a piece on classical pageant queens in D.C. and surrounding areas. Yes, that would work.

She ignored the ball of doubt in her gut. It was time to be strong.

A deep breath, and Taylor left the car.

Her heart was a slow drum in her ears. She walked up the driveway toward the front porch, where an old rocking chair creaked in the wind. An axe poked out of a stump on the front lawn next to piles of haphazardly chopped logs. Only the sound of crickets trilling filled the air—if Jeremiah was inside, he was being dead silent.

Taylor's feet creaked against the porch when she walked across it, and she held her breath, as though afraid she'd alerted him and he'd appear with a shotgun, branding her a trespasser. It was late—almost 10:30 p.m.—after all, and unorthodox for anyone to be visiting at this hour. But Taylor was convinced she could talk her way through it. She had to.

It felt like an eternity had passed, but she reached the front door. Her palms were sweaty as she rang the doorbell. Still, silence, until—

The door opened.

A broad-chested man, at least six-foot-three inches tall, stood behind the screen. He was only in his thirties, but he gave off a much more weathered appearance. He looked down at Taylor beneath bushy eyebrows with eyes so dark they were nearly black. His skin was leathery, sunburnt, and he wore a plaid shirt tucked into a pair of jeans, work boots on his feet.

Work boots.

The foot print she'd found at Jacob Gregory's crime scene flared in her mind. The hairs on the back of her neck rose, and every instinct told her to leave.

But she didn't.

"Can I help you?" he asked. His voice was rougher, gruffer than Taylor had expected. If he was her guy—his gruff, masculine appearance contradicted how she'd pictured the killer. After all, someone obsessed with dresses and makeup, she expected to be more like Monet or Johansson.

Snapping out of it, Taylor realized he was still staring. "Hello, sir," she said. "Sorry to bother you so late. Would this happen to be the residence of, ah—" She hesitated as the fear seeped in, but finished with, "Matilda Swanson?"

"Yes," he said, "but my mother passed away last week."

"I heard… I'm so sorry," Taylor said. "Actually, I'm with *The Washington Post*. We're doing a piece on beauty pageant queens in D.C. and the surrounding area, and Mrs. Swanson happened to be last on my list. Do you mind if I ask you a few questions about your mother?"

"It's late," Jeremiah said. "Come back another time."

He went to close the door, but Taylor, in a panic, cut in with: "Please. It's been a long day. I promise I'll only be a minute."

He watched her for a moment, before he finally said, "Fine. Come in."

Jeremiah pushed open the screen door and held it for Taylor. Against her better judgement, she stepped into the house.

It was hot and dank inside, and an odor Taylor couldn't place emanated off Jeremiah as she passed under his arm—like he hadn't bathed in some time. A film of dust collected over Victorian-esque furniture. Pictures of Matilda in her youth hung on the walls, and more framed photos were displayed on the console table by the front door.

There wasn't a single picture of Jeremiah anywhere.

"So," Jeremiah said, wiping his hands on his jeans. His palms were slightly blackened. "Why don't you come in and make yourself at home?"

He suddenly seemed warmer than before. Taylor, with a slight smile, nodded. As he led her into the house, they passed by a closed white door. Taylor glanced at it, wondering what was behind, but continued behind Jeremiah to the living room. He gestured for her to sit at a lone loveseat while he took the couch. Beside the coffee table was an empty rocking chair, and an old box TV—so old it still had antennas—was positioned against the wall.

Taylor snapped herself back into the moment. Right—she was a reporter. She pulled out a spare notepad and pen from her jacket pocket and readied it to "take notes."

"So, um—"

"Jeremiah," he cut in. "Nice to meet you. Mother's never had anyone report on her. Not in a long time."

"Thanks," Taylor said. "I won't take up too much of your time. Why don't you start by telling me about your mother? Who was she? More specifically, who was she when she was at the height of her pageant career?"

"As you can see, my mother was quite the show woman." He gestured to the photos surrounding them. "She was much more about beauty than work, which, of course, was hard for us after my father died. No more farm work." Jeremiah had a strange dialect—likely from his years of homeschooling, though his vocabulary seemed fine.

"I'm sorry to hear that," Taylor said. "Did she continue to compete after he passed away?"

"Oh, yeah. For a few years. Things began to go down once she turned thirty. Too old for pageants, or so they said."

Taylor nodded. Matilda would have been in her early thirties twenty-five years ago, when the reports of Jeremiah's bruises were reported. Maybe feeling "too old" to be beautiful caused her to break.

"My mother worked very hard as a single mom," Jeremiah said. "She didn't have a job other than being a pageant queen, but she worked really hard to take care of me and raised me all by herself. That alone made her my hero. Make sure you write that down. That's how I want her to be remembered: as a hero."

Nothing on him seemed to indicate he felt any resentment for her. Maybe there was no abuse here. Maybe Taylor had it wrong, yet again, and Jeremiah was just a simple farm boy dealt some hard cards in life. Maybe those bruises the teacher allegedly saw were never real.

Something thumped in the other room.

The chills returned to Taylor in full force. Jeremiah didn't seem to notice the sound, but if Taylor had to guess the direction, it came from the door they'd passed on the way to the living room.

Shit. I need to find a way in there.

But there was no way she'd be able to get past Jeremiah, who was a brick wall of a man.

In a matter of seconds, she concocted a plan. She'd have to act fast.

All at once, Taylor faked a coughing fit, hacking into her elbow. Jeremiah stiffened.

"Are you all right?" he asked calmly.

"Yes," Taylor stammered, regaining her composure. "Maybe some water?"

The moment Jeremiah stood up and went toward the kitchen, Taylor was on the move.

She darted toward the closed white door. With no hesitation, she opened it to find a dark room with a hallway and two openings. From one came a slight light. Taylor hurried inside and followed the light, just a few steps into the room.

Then, everything stood still.

A man—wearing a purple dress—was tied to a chair beneath a single lightbulb. He had fallen over and was on the floor. Blood oozed down his face, but he was breathing. And when he saw her, his eyes went wide, and he attempted to speak through his gag.

Taylor didn't have a fraction of a second to think before footsteps pounded the floor behind her.

Her hand flew toward her gun, but it was too late. Jeremiah's strong hangs grabbed her by the arms and lifted her into the air. Taylor's foot flew backwards, right into his gut, and he made a retching noise as he dropped her.

Swiftly, she removed her gun, but before she even could aim it, Jeremiah's giant hand was on her arm. He tried to pry the gun away from her, and she did everything in her power to keep it in her grip—but he was too strong. The gun dropped, and as Jeremiah forced Taylor to the floor, it got kicked away.

She wrestled out of his grasp and managed to get herself on her feet, now squaring up against him with only her years of training as a weapon.

But she had never faced off against someone so large.

Jeremiah's eyes had become empty, like two soulless pits of oil. His brows were furrowed, and he looked at her with nothing but a tempered rage. She was his prey. And her only hope was the gun, now in the corner of the room.

Beside them, the victim writhed against the chair he was still tied to, attempting to make more noise, but all of his sounds were muffled.

"It's over, Jeremiah," Taylor said, but her voice came out shaky and weak.

Just then, he dove for her. She ducked beneath him, letting him fall forward, then darted for the gun. As her hand reached toward it, her legs were pulled back by a force as strong as gravity. Jeremiah dragged her back, and as he tried to lift her, she kicked him in the groin. He grunted in pain, and Taylor scrambled for the gun again.

But this time, when Jeremiah grabbed her, he flipped her over onto her back and pinned her down.

His hands wrapped firmly around her throat, and no matter how hard Taylor kicked, clawing at his meaty arms, his grip only tightened.

Taylor never thought she'd die like this. When she pictured herself losing a battle on the job, she figured it'd be from a fatal gunshot, not having the life strangled from her by an unfairly large man. But she knew, as she struggled beneath Jeremiah's tremendous strength, that she had lost this fight.

She thought of her parents, back home in Baltimore, losing another daughter.

She thought of Angie, wherever she was. Maybe Taylor would see her soon.

Her head began to feel full, yet light, like it was about to pop.

Jeremiah's face above her faded in and out of white. And before she could even have a final thought, she slipped away, into the dark…

CHAPTER TWENTY FIVE

A loud noise bellowed around Taylor's head. The pressure lifted from her neck, and air struggled to enter her lungs. She gasped as though she'd been trapped underwater.

She couldn't see. She could barely even *feel.* Everything was black, and she kept gasping and gasping, like breathing through a tiny straw.

Slowly, the room materialized before her, but she could only make out vague shapes like distorted amoebas. Sounds bled into her ears—grunts and ragged breaths. The shapes became clearer, but the pain throughout her body rendered her unable to move, even as her cognizance returned through a hazy sheet of glass.

I'm not dead.

Something had stopped Jeremiah from killing her. But Taylor had no idea what. Vision still blurry, she squinted hard to see the scene in front of her. She'd lost too much oxygen to her brain and it was fighting to accept she hadn't been killed. But as her eyes returned to focus, the unmistakable shape of Calvin Scott appeared before her.

You came. Taylor allowed herself a fraction of a second to feel relieved—but she quickly realized now wasn't the time. Her partner had come to save her—but now, he was in trouble.

Calvin's gun was out, but like with Taylor, Jeremiah's giant hand was wrapped around Calvin's forearm, forcing him to point the gun upward. Jeremiah squeezed so hard that the gun dropped from Calvin's hand, and then he swung his huge fist right into Calvin's face. The agonizing sound of bone cracking filled the room.

Still delirious, Taylor struggled to stand. She had to do something. And she had to do it fast.

My gun! Taylor's mind was still broken, but every instinct in her screamed to find her weapon. It was the only thing that could save them. But no matter her resolve, she tripped over her own feet and fell to the ground. Her skull continued to throb as she remained on all fours, feeling helpless and powerless.

Looking over her shoulder, she saw Jeremiah knock Calvin in the head again, hard.

This time, he collapsed to the ground.

And Jeremiah's sights were back on her.

His hulking frame stormed toward her. The fear shocked her back to life. Taylor scrambled backwards, feeling all over the cold, concrete ground for any sign of her gun.

Damn it! Where is it?

This might be the end. Calvin was down. No one was coming to help her.

Jeremiah was too strong. She'd underestimated him. She should have known that someone capable of such villainous crimes wouldn't do down without a fight.

But then she felt it: the cool metal of her gun.

She didn't think. She just grabbed it, pointed it forward, and shot.

The sound resonated throughout the small room and bounced off the walls. It pierced Taylor's brain, disorienting her even further. Her vision blanked again. A deep silence filled the room beneath the ringing in Taylor's ears.

Did I get him? Is he down?

She wanted Jeremiah Swanson behind bars, not dead. But she also wanted to go home to Ben tonight. To apologize for being so reckless. She wanted to save Calvin Scott's life—and her own. And if that meant killing Jeremiah, she'd do it.

But when the rough feeling of his hands gripped her throat again, she realized she hadn't defeated him at all.

His tremendous weight pressed upon her, and once more, she gasped for air, but nothing came. This time was different, though—his grip wasn't as strong. Warm liquid dripped onto Taylor's jacket, and she managed to look up to see an open wound leaking red from his shoulder. *I got him!*

Jeremiah's face was contorted in rage—and pain. With the last bit of her strength, Taylor shot her knee upward and slammed it into his groin. Jeremiah retched and loosened his grip enough for Taylor to push him off her. Jeremiah, still in pain, stood, holding his bleeding shoulder.

Finally on even ground, Taylor wasn't about to let him get the best of her again. When Jeremiah lunged forward, she dodged him. Another lunge. Another dodge. They were like two wild animals—him mangy and deranged, her more like prey trying to outsmart the beast.

Jeremiah gripped his bleeding shoulder and seethed at Taylor. He let out a bloodcurdling, animalistic shout and spat on the floor. Near them, the man he'd bound and gagged whimpered. Taylor and Jeremiah circled each other slowly.

Go ahead, make another move, she wanted to say. He was weak now—still terrifying, but weak. And Taylor's adrenaline was high. This was life or death for everyone in the room—but if Jeremiah went at her again, she knew how she'd take him down. She didn't want him dead—she wanted him alive, rotting in a prison cell.

His skin, leathery and dark from days in the sun, was turning pale. Blood oozed down his arm, leaking through his fingers as he held the wound. He wouldn't last much longer. And he must have known that too, because using all his strength, he lunged at Taylor one last time.

This time, she used a double-leg takedown to send him flying toward the concrete, chest first. And when his massive body slammed down, he writhed in pain, giving Taylor a window to straddle his back. She slapped cuffs on him as he groaned, a pool of blood forming around his body.

"Jeremiah Swanson," Taylor began, "you have the right to remain silent. Anything you say can and will be—"

As Taylor bent over, a sharp pain stabbed her chest and knocked the wind from her lungs. It was like all of her air had been cut off and she was being stabbed over and over, right through the ribcage.

Something's wrong. She opened her mouth to speak again. No words came out.

She tried to breathe, but it was as though Jeremiah was choking her again. She couldn't catch a breath.

The pain in her chest grew, becoming so sharp it was like the knives were stabbing her heart now too.

Then, everything went black.

CHAPTER TWENTY SIX

A white light surrounded Taylor. Her body was numb, and for a moment, she felt like she was floating out on the ocean beneath a cerulean sky. Slowly, a sound bled in. A steady beep. A ceiling materialized above her, and as her eyes fluttered open, the last memory she had before the blackout emerged.

The pain. *Jeremiah Swanson.*

Taylor jolted upright and gasped for air.

"Hey, slow down!" someone shouted.

As Taylor's eyes adjusted to the light, she took in her surroundings—tubes connected to her arms, a white-walled room, a soft bed she was lying in.

I'm in the hospital?

Although her heart pounded, she relaxed enough to see the person hovering beside her bed. It was Calvin Scott, half of his face covered in galaxy-like bruises, his left eye completely shut.

"Sage, you need to take it easy," he said, voice steady.

"Calvin?" she stammered. "What happened? Where—"

"Relax. I'll explain everything." Calvin sat back down in the chair beside her bed.

Taylor pressed her back against the plush pillow behind her, mind racing. How did they get here? What the hell was that excruciating pain before she passed out?

Most importantly, what happened to Jeremiah?

"Your husband's here too," Calvin said. "I just sent him down about ten minutes ago to get some food for you. The doctors said you should wake up soon."

"Tell me what happened with Jeremiah Swanson," was all Taylor could say.

Calvin sighed. "Right to the point, huh? Well, as you must've seen, that massive guy got the best of me. I was knocked out for a bit. When I came to, apparently you'd already done the hard work of cuffing him. But you were also passed out. Jeremiah was writhing around, trying to get out of his cuffs when more backup arrived. That's when we transported you to the hospital."

"I shot him," Taylor uttered. "Is he…"

"He's fine. Lost some blood, but fine. We have him in custody."

Taylor let out a breath and melted into the hospital bed. *We got him.* Jeremiah Swanson had actually been caught, and for the first time since she moved to Pelican Beach, Taylor felt every muscle in her body relax.

Of course, until Calvin, with irritation in his voice, said, "For fuck's sake, Sage…"

Taylor looked at him. His face was twisted with a mix of anger and hurt. But mostly anger.

"Why didn't you wait for backup?" he went on. "You could've been *killed.* I swear, if I'd arrived even a minute later, we wouldn't be here. If you'd just waited for me to check my damn phone, we could've gone over it together."

Despite the situation, Taylor couldn't help but smile. She appreciated his concern, but she was in a blissful state right now, grateful this whole ordeal was permanently finished. And sure, she was in the hospital, but she was still *alive.* "I'm sorry, Agent Scott. I tried to call you, but… I was in too deep. I couldn't just walk away. I had this feeling there was another victim, and if I didn't go at that moment, he could've been killed. Maybe it sounds crazy… but I trusted my intuition."

He laughed once and looked away. "And you were right. The man whose life you saved is named Carl Miller, and he's currently in recovery. Swanson was going to kill him that night."

Taylor relaxed her head against the soft hospital pillow. "I'm glad he's okay."

Calvin ran his hang along the back of his neck. "Yeah, and… well, I shouldn't be giving you shit. I'm sorry I didn't believe you before. I should've at least looked into things further, out of respect for you, but…"

"It's okay." Taylor smiled. "You were tired, and you wanted to go home. Most people like to rest."

"Most people," Calvin said. "Now you're the one who's been sleeping for ages."

"How long have I been out for?" She noted the sunlight leaking in through the window, giving the room an ethereal glow.

"All night," Calvin said. "It's about eleven right now."

Silence filled the room, only the steady beeping of Taylor's heart on the monitor to occupy the space. But it wasn't uncomfortable.

Taylor had spent so much time blocking her emotions from her partner, as she blocked from everyone. But she wanted him to know how much she appreciated him.

"You're a good partner, Scott," Taylor said, smiling. His eyes snapped to hers. "Thanks for having my back."

Smiling back, he nodded, but was clearly flustered at the compliment. "Hey, of course."

Before the awkward silence could seep in, the door opened, and a woman in her late thirties wearing a doctor's coat stepped into the room. A lanyard hung around her neck, and she carried a clipboard, her long red hair tied back in a bun. When she saw Taylor awake, she exclaimed, "Oh, good, you're up!"

Calvin stood up and nodded at the doctor, then Taylor, with a tight-lipped smile. "I'll give you some privacy." With that, he left the room.

Taylor met the doctor's curious green eyes.

"Well, Mrs. Sage," the doctor said, "you're what I'd like to call a 'true survivor.'"

"Was it that close of a call?" Taylor asked.

The doctor smiled warmly. "Don't worry, we expect you to make a full recovery. While you were unconscious, we performed a full body scan. You suffered from a broken rib, which led to some internal bleeding and a punctured lung."

Taylor gritted her teeth, but it wasn't surprising. Jeremiah had a strength unmatched by any man she'd been forced to fight before. His fists had been like mallets. She wasn't surprised he'd managed to break a rib.

She hated feeling weak. But she also wasn't stupid. A one-on-one face-off against that guy was just unfair, and she reminded herself that she needed to be extra careful from now on. This was a reminder of her own mortality, and how easy it would have been for Jeremiah Swanson to steal her life from her, as he'd stolen from so many.

An overwhelming feeling of elation washed through her. She had a second chance at life. She wouldn't waste it.

The doctor continued, "Thankfully, we didn't find any permanent damage to your internal organs, aside from the existing damage to your uterus."

Taylor froze. What *existing damage?*

But the doctor went on, chipper, as if she hadn't just dropped a bomb. "That's why I called you a true survivor, Mrs. Sage. I saw on your medical records that you suffered a serious gunshot wound early in your career. And now you've survived another serious assault. I'm happy to say that this time, there's nothing to worry about—you should be fully healed within a few weeks."

"Hold on," Taylor cut in. Her head hurt, and she was still caught up on what the doctor had said about the gunshot. "What existing damage to my uterus?"

The doctor's face dropped. She blinked, quiet, before she finally said, "I… I thought you knew."

"I knew I was shot," Taylor said, "but what damage to my uterus?"

The panic was beginning to set in. She'd never heard this before. It had to be an error.

"Oh, my…," the doctor cleared her throat. Now, a guilty look took over her freckled face. Taylor's mouth went dry with anticipation, until the doctor continued, "I'm so sorry I have to tell you this. It's highly unnerving that the doctors didn't say anything before, but…" She averted her eyes. "Taylor, the damage to your uterus is extremely severe. It was clear to my team and me just by looking at it that you will never be able to conceive children."

Taylor turned to stone. The doctor's words spiraled around her head.

Never be able to conceive.

Never have children.

There was no way. Images of the life she'd once pictured with Ben flared into her mind. The phantom children in their homes at their new house. The phantom daughter she'd imagined dropping off at Winning Princesses in D.C.

Taylor had dealt with her own doubts. But to have the option ripped away from her—it couldn't be real.

"I'll leave you alone to process this," the doctor quietly said. "I'm so sorry. We'll check back in a little while." With a bow, she ducked out of the room and closed the door, leaving Taylor to face her thoughts head-on.

How was she going to tell Ben? Since their first date, Ben made it clear that he wanted a family someday. She did too. It wasn't just a small conversation, but it was one they'd gotten out of the way early, so not to waste each other's time.

And now, all these years later, she was being told it could *never* happen?

She clutched at her pounding head as tears burned her eyes. Taylor couldn't hold back the tears—she broke into a full-blown sob. *This can't be real. Please, somebody wake me up!*

But no matter how much she wished to be away, she was still in that hospital room with this new knowledge, still crying, feeling pathetic and alone.

Taylor allowed herself to cry, but only for a moment. She'd never been one to shed many tears, and Ben had only seen her cry a small handful of times, mostly out of frustration. She couldn't allow herself to feel weak. A cold, steely sensation came over her.

If this was what she had to face next, then she would have to do it. Maybe she'd find a way out. Maybe a miracle could happen.

Just as she was trying to figure out a mental gameplan, the door opened and Ben burst in. *Shit.* He was the last person she wanted to see right now, as seeing his joyful face only tempted her with more tears. But she stifled them down.

Before Taylor could utter a word, Ben threw his arms around her. His warm, heavy, and familiar weight cocooned her. Once more, Taylor wanted to cry.

"Taylor, I'm so glad you're okay," Ben said against her ear.

He pulled away, and his brown eyes met hers, looking happier than ever.

"Thanks," Taylor said. "I'm sorry if I scared you."

"Scared me?!" Ben exclaimed. "I nearly had a heart attack pacing around. The doctors were so busy, and your partner had to calm me down. I was a wreck."

Taylor pictured Calvin calming down a hysterical Ben. She made a mental note to thank him for that later too.

"I'm just glad this is all over," Ben said, sitting down in the chair. He grabbed Taylor's hands with his, surrounding them in his warmth. He smoothed his hand along her finger, over her wedding ring. "Sweetheart, when I was scared that I was going to lose you, all I could think about was our perfect future being ripped away from us."

Taylor's chest stuttered. Perfect future. Of course, that meant having children.

Holding back more tears, she said, "You're not still mad at me? About the other day?"

"No, no," he said. "I'm the one who should apologize. I was being a selfish jerk. I know how much your work means to you and how important this case was. And it's no surprise that my wife was the one who caught the killer and saved another life. I should have believed in you."

Taylor allowed her head to fall to the side, focusing on the wall beside her, unable to stand the exuberant look in Ben's eyes. But he only gripped her hands tighter.

"I lost sight of why I fell in love with you in the first place," he said. "I was so blinded by my own selfishness that I forgot it was your tenacious spirit that made me want to marry you. It's your strong sense of justice and empathy that I *know* will make you an amazing mother."

"Ben, stop," she said. Her heart was breaking with every word. She'd never seen Ben with so much resolve. And she couldn't stand the thought of telling him what the doctor had just told her.

"No," he said, laughing, "I know you don't like it when I get all mushy. But it's true! You're a fantastic woman, Taylor. I'm so glad you're okay." Once more, he leaned over the bed and hugged her.

And maybe it was selfish, but Taylor allowed herself to melt into his warmth, to feel comforted by his familiar smell. She couldn't stand the idea of breaking his heart.

So for now, she would keep this secret to herself.

CHAPTER TWENTY SEVEN

Taylor walked briskly into the Quantico headquarters, feeling ten times lighter than she had the last time she'd walked through these doors. She nodded at a few familiar faces, who smiled and waved, as she made her way through the sleek hallways. A full two weeks had passed since she'd last stepped foot in this building, and even though she'd only been active here for a short time, it felt familiar to be back. It felt right.

In the fallout of Jeremiah's arrest, Taylor was forced to stay in the hospital for several days, then returned home to take a full week off work—chief's orders. As much as Taylor had hated not being put immediately on her next mission, she'd decided to let herself relax at home with Ben and get the rest of their house unpacked. It was the least she could do for her husband after the scare she'd given him.

Plus, Taylor had to admit, taking some time off to relax had been, well, fun. She and Ben had some movie and wine nights, and Taylor got to learn all about the hotel Ben was working on. Her parents even came for a visit, grateful that Taylor was alive, well, and recovering. Her dad made pancakes for dinner and they spent an evening feeling like a 'normal' family.

Of course, while all this joy was happening, there had also been the moments of guilt. The cloud looming over Taylor's head that she tried to push away, but it always lingered with her.

She hadn't yet found the right moment to tell Ben the truth about what she'd learned at the hospital—that she might never bear children. Maybe she was still in denial herself, as she hadn't booked a full examination. Maybe another doctor could tell her something different. But she was also afraid they'd only confirm what the hospital had told her.

As Taylor turned a corner, she pushed those thoughts aside. Steven Winchester's hulking frame stood outside of the briefing room, waiting for her. And when they met, he offered her a hand, which she firmly shook.

"Special Agent Sage, nice to see you back," Winchester said. "But I want to make one thing clear—you're not here to work, got it? This is just an update."

"Got it," Taylor mumbled. She'd been asking Winchester to let her come in and review the case files since she was discharged from the hospital, but Winchester had quite literally forced her to take that (much-needed) time off. Today, she'd finally convinced him she was well enough to come in for at least a visit and learn everything that happened after Swanson's arrest.

"Once you've made a full recovery, we can get you back in the field," Winchester told her. "Come on, Agent Scott is waiting."

They went into the briefing room, where Calvin was sitting on the table next to an open laptop. He stood at attention when Taylor entered and offered her a hand. They'd only spoken briefly on the phone over the past two weeks, but Taylor was happy to see him well. They shook hands and shared a quick, but appreciative smile.

"Well, you wanted to know what we found out about Swanson, so here goes," Winchester said, going on the laptop. He clacked away as Taylor and Calvin stood back. "After the arrest, we searched his house and found… a lot of grisly shit, to say the least."

Calvin nodded, brows raised. "Oh yeah. You could say that."

Taylor wished she had been involved in the search and had been able to see all the evidence. As morbid as it was, understanding a killer's psyche was what made her job so fascinating, and she wanted to unearth those elements herself. But this would have to do. At least now, she could have some closure.

"There were a lot of home movies," Winchester said. "Some I think will help us understand why this guy did what he did. Take a look. And brace yourself. It's… disturbing."

A video loaded on the screen. It showed a child—maybe seven or eight—standing in a living room, wearing a purple dress. He was a male with short brown hair. Taylor immediately recognized the floral couches behind him. She could practically smell the dusty, mildewy stench of the home now, and it made her stomach churn, remembering all the pain that came with her visit there.

This was Jeremiah Swanson as a child, in that very same farm house.

On the screen, Jeremiah stepped back and forth, as if in some sort of clumsy dance. Even for a child, he appeared larger than most kids his age.

Behind the camera, the grating voice of a woman scraped Taylor's ears.

"No, no! Not like that!"

Jeremiah's eyes appeared devastated. But he didn't speak.

"Again!" the woman—who must have been his mother—shouted. *"And sing, I told you to sing!"*

Awkwardly stepping back and forth, Jeremiah mumbled a tune so low, it was barely audible.

The lower half of the woman shuffled onto the screen. She was also wearing a dress, lacy and silky. Her face wasn't visible. Jeremiah cowered away, as though he knew what was coming.

She slapped him hard across the face. The *smack* resonated through the speakers of the laptop. Taylor covered her mouth in shock.

On camera, Jeremiah fell back and was instantly in tears.

"Again!" his mother screamed.

As he struggled to stand, crying and holding his face, Winchester stopped the video. Silence filled the room as he shut the laptop.

"That should probably tell you enough," Winchester said. "Pretty nasty stuff."

Taylor didn't know what to say. The man she'd fought with—who had killed all those men—was a monster. There was no doubt about that. But the child in the video was innocent. He didn't deserve that treatment. And Taylor couldn't help but think that Jeremiah, himself, was a victim too, even if he did belong behind bars.

"I was able to talk to him while you were in recovery," Calvin said. "He was a stonewall, more or less. I didn't get anything. Not a word about how he chose his victims and why."

Taylor had been thinking about this for the past two weeks. She'd forced herself to stay patient, to follow orders for once and rest up, but now that she had Winchester in front of her, she had to ask.

"Sir," she said, "I'd like to visit Swanson in prison myself. See if I can get anything out of him."

Winchester just sighed. "Sage, you're still recovering. Agent Scott tried to get the guy to talk, but he wouldn't."

"And he's a great interviewer," Taylor said, "but I'm the one who faced off against him. I'm the one he was talking to before things turned south. If I can at least get him to tell us a bit about why he did this, and how he chose his victims, then maybe it will give the families closure."

Winchester glanced at Calvin, as though asking what he thought, but Calvin just shrugged and said, “She’s the one who really got him, Chief. If Taylor wants to see him, why stop her?”

“Because I want her to get some damn rest,” Winchester said, then sighed again, meeting Taylor’s expectant gaze. “Fine. But you’re still on leave until further notice. Got it?”

Taylor smiled. “Got it.”

***

A massive, barred door slammed behind Taylor as she entered a room in the maximum-security prison. She found herself in another small room, in front of another door, with the security guard who’d led her there.

“You’ll be protected by glass,” the security guard said, “but if you have any issues at all, there’s a button on the table. Press it and we’ll be in there in seconds.”

Taylor nodded. “Don’t worry. I can handle him.”

The guard nodded, and with that, opened the door. The light on the other side was near blinding for a moment, the sun coming in full blast through the grated windows. Taylor stepped inside, and the door shut behind her.

On the other side of the plexiglass divider, Jeremiah sat, his face shadowed, making his eyes look nearly black. A jolt of anxiety struck her. The last time she’d been alone with this man, he’d nearly choked the life out of her. She took comfort in the secured glass between them. Not even he would be strong enough to break free from this cage.

Hesitantly, Taylor took a seat, and that was when Jeremiah finally looked. His brown eyes were cold, emotionless, sending tingles up her spine.

“Jeremiah Swanson,” Taylor said. “Do you remember who I am?”

He said nothing. Just stared. But Taylor had looked into the eyes of many killers. He didn’t scare her, not anymore.

“My real name is Taylor Sage,” she continued. “I’m the federal agent who tracked you down. I suspected you were involved in the murders of the young men.”

Still, nothing. This guy really was a brick wall. Taylor realized she would have to crank it up if she wanted him to talk.

“I saw the videos my team recovered from your home,” Taylor said. “The videos of you and your mother.”

A hint of emotion flickered in his gaze, although he still did not speak.

"It's awful, what she did to you," Taylor said. "No child should have to go through that."

"My mother loved me," he cut in. His voice was deep, baritone, and angry.

"I'm sure she did," Taylor said carefully. She knew better than to antagonize him. Instead, she leaned forward and clasped her hands on the table, hoping to keep him calm. "I won't take up too much of your time. How did you choose your victims, Jeremiah? They had families, people who loved them. What were you trying to prove?"

He turned into a statue again, eyes trained firmly on Taylor.

"Was it because of how they looked?" Taylor pressed. "If so, how did you choose them? Was it just the wrong place at the wrong time? Or did you follow them beforehand?"

When he didn't answer again, Taylor couldn't help but sigh.

"Okay. If you won't tell me why you chose them, will you tell me about the dresses?" She kept her gaze firm. "Was it because your mother dressed you up?"

Once more, emotion leaked into his stony gaze. It seemed only mentions of his mother could get him to crack.

Taylor thought back to the idea of "overbearing expectations," and how on the video, his mother had been so displeased with his performance that she beat him.

"Were you trying to prove something to her, Jeremiah?" she asked.

He crossed his arms over his chest and closed his eyes, as though visually showing her that he was done talking. For good.

Clearly, this was a waste of time. Taylor understood why Calvin had given up. They could put him behind bars—but they couldn't force him to talk. With a sigh, Taylor stood and went to leave.

But as she was at the door, he said:

"Mother never thought I was pretty enough. I just wanted to find someone worthy of her. But none of them were."

His cold voice chilled Taylor to the core. She understood it now. Even after her death, Jeremiah was trying to please his mother, but since he had been deemed "too ugly," he must have chosen other men as victims—or "offerings." Which explained why all of the men were relatively young, in decent physical shape, and conventionally attractive.

It made Taylor sick, thinking back to that video she'd seen earlier. How could someone have a child and treat them so cruelly? She ran her hand over her abdomen. *It doesn't feel fair.*

Now isn't the time, she reminded herself, looking at Jeremiah, although his eyes were downcast now. Maybe Taylor could press him more, try to get him to talk more… but she'd gathered enough. She had her answers.

And Jeremiah Swanson would stay behind bars forever. So for now, Taylor could go home to her husband and rest.

At least until the next job.

CHAPTER TWENTY EIGHT

An array of books spread on the living room floor before Taylor, Ben sitting cross-legged on the other side of the chaos. He wore an easygoing smile on his face, showing off his dimples, as he sorted one of Taylor's books into her pile. They'd always liked having their own separate bookshelves, mostly because the content was so wildly different—Ben, with his historical nonfiction, fantasy novels, and books on architecture, and Taylor, with her books on psychology, serial killers, and anatomy.

She liked seeing him happy. A beam of sunlight poured through their curtains and brightened Ben's smile. The house felt so lived in now, as opposed to a few weeks ago, and these books were the last to be sorted.

"At least you're home to help me with this mess," Ben muttered. "I'm telling you, I was scared I'd have to organize these myself!"

Taylor smiled and placed one of Ben's books in his pile. "Well, we put it off for too long."

He shot her a flirty glance with a devious smirk. Taylor knew that look. He said, "That's fine with me. At least we're not putting off that *other* thing anymore."

Taylor blushed. She felt like an awful person, but she had been more open to sex with him lately… mostly because she knew she couldn't get pregnant.

I have to tell him.

But how? When?

And then, a paralyzing thought:

Will he leave me?

Subconsciously, Taylor had feared that most of all this whole time. But she hadn't given the thought room to grow roots.

No... he wouldn't leave me.

We said vows.

She thought back to their wedding day. How happy she had been. She never thought she'd find love, but she found it in Ben Chambers. Her 'forever.'

Taylor's stomach churned. Lately, when she felt anxious, she swore it felt like the wound on her uterus was opening up all over again. Now, more than ever, she regretted what she did all those years ago that led to her being shot.

Just a few weeks ago, she'd exhibited that same recklessness when she went to Jeremiah Swanson's farmhouse without backup.

Have I grown at all? she wondered. How could she be so recklessly brave—or 'stupid,' as Calvin would probably say—and yet be too much of a coward to simply tell the man she married the truth? Somehow, the idea of going to work and facing off against a stone-cold killer was less terrifying.

"You okay, honey?" Ben's voice cut in.

Taylor's eyes snapped to him. To his easy smile. And she forced one back, saying, "Yeah, of course. Just thinking about work."

"As per usual," he joked. "I love having you home, so I can't complain that they haven't called you back in yet…"

Ben kept talking, but his words faded into the background noise in her head. She watched him as he smiled while he talked, so casual, so comfortable.

As Taylor focused on him while he talked, her heartbeat began to increase. Tingles of anxiety jolted through her.

She couldn't put this off anymore. Ben needed to know the truth.

Even if he leaves you?

Pinching her eyes shut, she shook that thought away. It was time for her to have faith in her husband—in their marriage, and in herself. Taylor wouldn't have chosen someone who would walk away from their commitment because of something out of her control.

She sucked in a breath and opened her eyes, staring at Ben intently. "Ben, I have to tell you something."

He met her stare with a clueless innocence. "Yes, honey?"

"I—"

The ring of a cellphone cut her off.

"Oh, shoot, sorry," Ben said, sliding his phone from the pocket of his jeans. His face lit up at the screen "It's work! I have to take this. One sec."

Ben got up and paced into the other room, talking into the phone. Taylor's chest sank deep into her stomach. She had finally built up the nerve, for it to all be taken away?

Moments later, Ben returned. Smiling eagerly. "They need me in today to go over some blueprints. That okay, honey?"

Taylor nodded, although her throat was tight. "Of course. Your work is important."

He offered her a hand and pulled her to her feet. They hugged and she relaxed against his chest. Maybe this was a sign she should wait a bit longer to tell Ben the truth.

And if Ben was leaving her alone, then there was one more person she wanted to speak to…

***

Miriam Belasco's shop was becoming more and more familiar to Taylor with every visit. As Taylor approached the doors, she checked over her shoulder, onto the quiet downtown street, as if to make sure she wasn't being followed.

She carried more than one secret with her lately—she had still never told anyone, not even Ben, about Belasco's inadvertent involvement the case. And she hadn't been back to visit since the time Belasco had given her the cards that made her believe there was some sort of parental connection with the case, which, of course, ended up being spot on.

As Taylor went up to the doors of the shop, a young couple left at the same time and nearly bumped into her. Taylor jumped back as they moved past her. Belasco was waving them off from inside the shop, and when her eyes fell on Taylor, her brows shot up.

"Mrs. Sage! It's you again!" Belasco exclaimed. "It's been so long; I was beginning to think you'd never return."

Taylor swallowed the lump in her throat. "Were you expecting me to?"

"I had an idea." Belasco winked and held the door open more. "Why don't you come in? I'll give you a reading, on the house."

Taylor hesitated, maybe on instinct. But at this point, she had to admit—this stuff wasn't *all* bullshit. Maybe part of her had always believed that, considering what happened right before she got shot the first time, back when Jeremy's sister had dragged her into a tarot reading. Maybe Taylor had always been so hesitant because she was afraid it *was* real. And although she wasn't one hundred percent convinced that she believed in psychics, or cosmic fate, or anything like that, she was starting to believe in cosmic *coincidence,* and maybe somehow, Belasco and her cards knew things Taylor didn't.

Either way, seeing Belasco didn't hurt, and she wanted to know if the cards could tell her anything about what might happen when she returned to work. So Taylor stepped into the shop, surrounded by the smell of burning incense.

Belasco stood with her hands clasped over her lap, a pleased smile on her red-painted lips, reminding Taylor of a wise, ancient shaman, rather than the scam artist she'd initially interpreted her as. The fact that Belasco had never asked her for money only reinforced that idea. Although today, Taylor intended on paying, at least for the woman's time.

"Right this way," Belasco said, and Taylor followed her behind the purple curtain, to the same table she'd now sat at twice.

The cards were already there, waiting. Belasco took her side of the table, and Taylor reluctantly took hers.

As Belasco shuffled the cards, she said, "So, what made you decide to come back?"

Taylor bit her tongue. Due to confidentiality, she couldn't give out specifics on the case. But she figured Belasco had earned a general idea.

"Those cards you read me before… they helped me on a case." *And maybe they can help my personal life too.*

"Oh?" Belasco asked like she wasn't surprised at all. "That's interesting! Might I ask how?"

"I can't share the details, but I will say, the words and meanings behind the cards helped get my brain working in the right direction, on more than one occasion." Taylor clammed up. Thanking people wasn't easy for her, but she said, "Thanks. I appreciate it."

A smile curled at Belasco's lips. "My pleasure. Are you working a case again today, and that's why you're here?"

"No, I've been off work for a bit, but I'm returning soon," Taylor paused. "I guess I just want some good fortune." *Or bad, if it has to be that way. At least I'll know.*

"Let's see what the cards have to say," Belasco said, sorting them into three piles. She met Taylor's stare. "Are you ready?"

Taylor nodded, thinking, *Please don't give me another 'Death' card...*

Belasco flipped the first card. Taylor sighed in relief when it was an image of two cups and some sort of snake.

"First, we have the Two of Cups, reversed," Belasco said. "This means imbalance, or broken communication, tension." Her eyes flashed at Taylor. "Apologies if I'm overstepping, but this is now the second time you've come alone…"

Taylor's throat tightened. She got what Belasco was getting at. Ben wasn't there. That wasn't because they were fighting, although there was tension in the relationship… and that huge secret Taylor was carrying.

"My husband and I are still together," Taylor said. "But I prefer to keep these meetings private, as I find them work-related."

Belasco nodded. "I understand. Let's move on." She flipped up the next card. "Next, we have the Four of Wands, reversed. This could allude to a lack of support, or a conflict at home."

Belasco studied Taylor, but Taylor averted her eyes. This was now the second card that could hint at some sort of marital issue, and the weight of that hung in the air. But Belasco didn't comment, just moved onto the final card.

"And finally…" She lifted up the card and flipped it. "We have the Three of Swords, upright. This could allude to grief… or to heartbreak."

More silence surrounded them as Taylor's palms grew sweaty. She hadn't even brought up her marriage, or given any sort of hint as to why she was really here—to get reassurance that telling Ben the truth would be okay. And yet the cards seemed to know anyway.

"So… what does it mean?" Taylor asked, afraid of the answer. Although she had a strong feeling she could interpret these herself.

"I can't say for sure," Belasco said. "But if I had to interpret them myself, I'd say…"

She drew a breath. Taylor's heart stuttered in her chest, until Belasco finally said:

"Someone important in your life is about to leave you."

NOW AVAILABLE!

DON'T BREATHE
(A Taylor Sage FBI Suspense Thriller —Book 2)

Victims of a new serial killer are turning up dead, chess pieces mysteriously left on their bodies. Brilliant FBI Special Agent Taylor Sage is determined to crack this one on her own, but when she hits a dead end, she must turn to the tarot reader for a clue—one that may hold the key, or may lead her right into a trap.

DON'T BREATHE is book #2 of a brand-new series by critically acclaimed and #1 bestselling mystery and suspense author Molly Black.

Taylor, in the midst of the case of her life, must also battle demons from her past: dark secrets from Taylor's past are threatening to bubble up—and possibly to end her marriage. Can she hold it together long enough to crack the case?

Or might she be the next victim?

A complex psychological crime thriller full of twists and turns and packed with heart-pounding suspense, the TAYLOR SAGE mystery series will make you fall in love with a brilliant new female protagonist and keep you turning pages late into the night.

Book #3 in the series—DON'T RUN—is now also available.

Molly Black

Debut author Molly Black is author of the MAYA GRAY FBI suspense thriller series, comprising six books (and counting); the RYLIE WOLF FBI suspense thriller series, comprising three books (and counting); and of the TAYLOR SAGE FBI suspense thriller series, comprising three books (and counting).

An avid reader and lifelong fan of the mystery and thriller genres, Molly loves to hear from you, so please feel free to visit www.mollyblackauthor.com to learn more and stay in touch.

BOOKS BY MOLLY BLACK

MAYA GRAY MYSTERY SERIES
GIRL ONE: MURDER (Book #1)
GIRL TWO: TAKEN (Book #2)
GIRL THREE: TRAPPED (Book #3)
GIRL FOUR: LURED (Book #4)
GIRL FIVE: BOUND (Book #5)
GIRL SIX: FORSAKEN (Book #6)

RYLIE WOLF FBI SUSPENSE THRILLER
FOUND YOU (Book #1)
CAUGHT YOU (Book #2)
SEE YOU (Book #3)

TAYLOR SAGE FBI SUSPENSE THRILLER
DON'T LOOK (Book #1)
DON'T BREATHE (Book #2)
DON'T RUN (Book #3)